FINAL REST

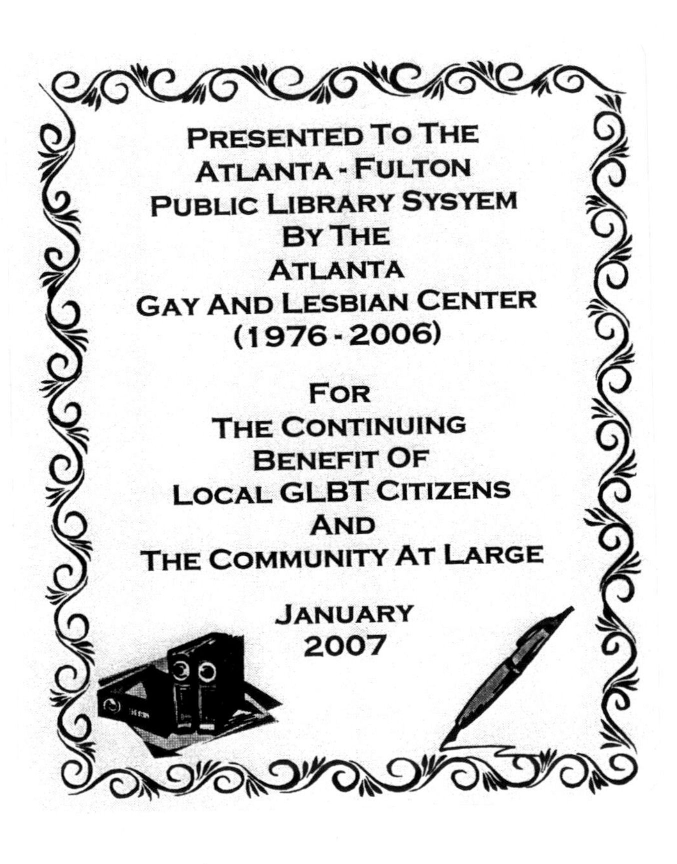
PRESENTED TO THE
ATLANTA - FULTON
PUBLIC LIBRARY SYSYEM
BY THE
ATLANTA
GAY AND LESBIAN CENTER
(1976 - 2006)
FOR
THE CONTINUING
BENEFIT OF
LOCAL GLBT CITIZENS
AND
THE COMMUNITY AT LARGE
JANUARY
2007

FINAL REST

A MYSTERY
BY MARY MORELL

spinsters ink
minneapolis

Final Rest: a mystery

First edition.
10-9-8-7-6-5-4-3-2

Spinsters Ink
P.O. Box 300170
Minneapolis, MN 55403

This is a work of fiction. Any similarity to persons living or dead is a coincidence.

Cover art by Zoe Van Horvitz
Production by: Melanie Cockrell, Joan Drury, Kay Hong, Kelly Kager, Lori Laughney, Carolyn Law, Mev Miller, Liz Tufte

Printed in the U.S.A. on acid-free paper.
Library of Congress Catalog Card Number: 93-84276
ISBN: 0-933216-94-7: $9.95

DEDICATION

This book holds at its heart, Ruby and Beatrice, two very special people who lived together and loved each other for fifty years. It is, however, dedicated to Ruby who, after Beatrice's death at 80, found the courage to love again.

ACKNOWLEDGEMENTS

I would like to acknowledge the persistent assistance of Anne Grey Frost who lends me her clear understanding of my characters and her repeated readings of dreck while I try to get to the good stuff. And my thanks go to Sheri White who distracted her, and to Eileen Cohen who distracted me.

Once again Emma Prophet has proven invaluable in her ME expertise. A special thanks goes to Dr. Bob who answered my drug questions endlessly and to Dr. Darlene who tasted digitalis so I didn't have to.

Despite terrible experiences with fire, illness and accident, the Wislen family have once again been very generous in their help. Thanks Anne, Lisa and Luke.

Judy, your knowledge of retirement living was essential. Thank you for sharing. The mistakes are all mine because I didn't listen up.

My friends Jan and Becky have again provided the feedback that always improves my mysteries.

The mentor of my youth, Lib Southerland, was my model for Min. I hope my thanks make it through the ether to her spirit. I miss you, Lib.

Finally I want to thank my writing pals who keep me paying attention to art: Beth Roll and Donna Fine.

Oh, and thanks to my brother Bill for the mug. I think I'll use it again sometime.

FINAL REST

SATURDAY

The sugar shaker set off its deep blue glass with a sterling silver lid and handle. Before she picked it up, Lorretta Millett admired it as she had almost every morning since her marriage to Laurence fifty-four years ago. It had been in his family for generations, brought over from England before the Civil War, or the War Between the States, as some still called it here in Alabama. Then it had been sent through the Straits of Magellan and up the Americas' coast to Oregon, backward across the Jubilee Trail to St. Louis and then to Enid, Oklahoma, to grace the table of the banker's new wife, her mother-in-law. The trip from Isabel's house to Lorretta's was only across the street. And now the sugar shaker had traveled with her, east to Alabama. Perhaps, she mused, it would complete the circle someday and return to England.

She firmly picked up the shaker, ignoring the slight tremor in her wrist. Very methodically, she covered her buttered toast with cinnamon–sugar, being careful not to spill any brownish grains over the edge of the toast onto the plate. When the cinnamon–sugar covered the toast evenly, Lorretta took a bite, then chewed twelve times before swallowing. She took another bite and did the same. She did not complete chewing the third bite. Her heart broke rhythm to her surprise and great annoyance. She rose to pull the emergency cord in her apartment wall. Before she could reach it, her heart faltered and stopped, leaving her body to crumple to the floor in dismay and death.

Twenty minutes later, there was a quiet knock at her door. After a few moments it was repeated slightly louder. Then a key turned in the lock. The door swung open wide enough that Lorretta's cooling body was clearly visible from the opening. The door closed.

SUNDAY

With her sweetheart beside her, Lucia strode up the geranium-bordered sidewalk with a spring in her step. The red flowers in her shirt set off the jet black of her short straight hair. For the first time in her homicide career, there were no active cases to work on. Of course, all the unsolved murders were still open, but there was nowhere to go with any of them. Saturday had also been her day off from the San Antonio Police Department, but she used it to finish up old paperwork. She sighed in the delight of wearing jeans two days in a row. "This is freedom," she thought as she led Amy past the balloon pop and dunking booths at the St. Anthony's Junior Seminary Fiesta. She glanced sideways to admire the sunlight caught in Amy's honey-brown hair. If it had been a more anonymous setting, she would have slid her arm around Amy's generous waist, perhaps crumpling the golden yellow sundress she was wearing, and proclaimed this woman her novia.

"Oh," Lucia said, "there's Tía Luz. Come on. Let's say hi." They ambled over to the group of Lucia's family that had clustered under a large oak near the soccer field. After a quarter of an hour of greetings, Tía Luz took Lucia's hand and then Amy's.

"Walk me up to the rummage sale," Tía Luz invited. "I need some cheap spoons for the after-school program. The kids won't use plastic any more. Imagine a second grader teaching me about the environment! What is the world coming to? Computers, video games. These kids know everything. It's amazing."

They went up the stairs to the huge front porch of the main building. Cardboard boxes filled with an incredible variety of household discards covered the worn outdoor carpeting. Blenders sat on disorderly stacks of Reader's Digest condensed novels. Chip and dip bowls curled inside straw baskets. Tía Luz started methodically with the first box to the left of the stairs and began her hunt.

"Go on. Poke around. If you find spoons, bring them to me." She waved Amy and Lucia off.

While most of the stacks contained stuff so familiar as to be banal, occasionally an item of mystery appeared. Lucia came across a pink terry cloth rabbit with a bell-shaped skirt and no lower body. She held it up for Amy's inspection.

"What do you think? A weird puppet?" She put her hand inside and tried to move it.

"Toilet paper cover," Amy said with great authority.

"How did you know? Secret psychologist information?"

"Sort of. I spent part of my practicum at an elder care center. They made them by the gross."

"Pretty gross, huh?" Lucia could not hide her own amusement at the terrible pun she had perpetrated.

"My goodness, Ramos, you're not going to sneak a new vice on me at this late date in our relationship, are you?" Amy narrowed her eyes in pretend sternness.

"It's a fit that only hits once or twice a year. I think of it as binge punning."

"Well, go inflict it on someone else. Talk to your tía. At least she's used to it," Amy said, gesturing with a bent curtain rod.

"I'd rather pester you," Lucia replied.

"I could use these coffee mugs in the office if they didn't have such a strange slogan. The 'St. Anthony Alumni Day' isn't bad. But what on earth is the 'Last Annual Bill Morell Roast'?"

"The old provincial of the Oblates. I guess they had those made for his farewell dinner. Looks like they made a few too many," Lucia said, gesturing at the stack of boxes, each of which held a dozen mugs. "Four dollars a box is cheap enough."

"Maybe I'll get a box later. I don't want to carry anything around." She moved on to the other side of the porch. "Here are some spoons."

"Great," Lucia said, scooping them up. She hurried back to the entrance and presented them for Tía Luz's approval.

"Done," Luz said. "Thanks, Lucita. Now I don't have to paw through any more boxes. Do you want to look at the silent auction inside?"

Amy, who had followed, looked at Lucia with a shrug.

"No thanks, Tía. I think we'll check out some of the other booths."

"Beto is doing the piñata booth behind the bingo tables. He'd love to see you," Tía Luz said, stepping inside the double doors.

"That okay?" Lucia asked.

"Sure," Amy replied.

The piñata hung from an orange plastic rope that had been tossed over a low branch of a live oak. Each arm of the red crepe-paper-covered star had eighteen-inch streamers of wide red and silver tinsel hanging down.

They sat in the shade of a nearby tree and watched as the line of children formed. First was a five-year-old whose dress matched the piñata. She looked all ready to cry when the two high school boys put the white handkerchief around her eyes. But she was distracted from her tears when they turned her around twice. One boy stood behind her and held her hands around the bat while the other untied the orange rope and lowered the piñata to her level.

"What's her name?" Amy asked. Lucia shrugged her unfamiliarity with the girl with the bat. "At last, someone who isn't a relative. I was beginning to think this was a family reunion disguised as a fiesta."

"Yeah. It kind of feels that way to me too. Do you want me to find out her name from Tía Luz? She'll know."

"No. Just idle curiosity. Why are those boys pulling the piñata out of the way? I thought the idea was to break it." Amy brushed a small brown ant off her wicker purse. She knew from experience that this variety didn't bite.

"Not right away. Each swing costs one ticket. They make it much harder for the older children so it will take longer. You want to give it a try? They'll probably keep it over your head." Her eyes looked hopefully at Amy.

"Why not? I don't really want any goldfish or iridescent shoelaces. And we have to spend these tickets somewhere." Amy grinned broadly. "Besides, I've been told I swing a bat like someone who hits at piñatas. I might even be good at it."

They brushed the leaves and dirt off their clothes and joined the line, their heads at least a foot higher than anyone else in line.

"Next," Tomás called. One by one, the giggling children took their turns. A very fat, pale boy got in a good hit and a few pieces of candy hit the ground.

"That would have broken it when I was a kid," Lucia murmured, almost to herself.

"Why?" Amy asked.

"They had clay pots inside then. Easier to break than paper. I don't know why they don't put them in anymore. Maybe it takes too long or costs too much."

"What do you put the candy in if there's no pot?"

"You cut a hole in the top and pull out some of the newspaper. That's all that's inside. You pour in the candy and stuff paper back in to make it solid. Some purists still buy little clay pots to put in, but it's a lot of trouble for something that's just going to be torn up." They moved closer to the head of the line. "This one is about ready to go."

The four shiny black braids of the identical black twins ahead of Lucia and Amy swung in unison as they walked up to take the next turn. "We only have one ticket left, so we want to do it together," one of them said.

"You can have one of mine," Amy offered.

"Sure, take it, kids. Then you can both hit," Tomás said.

There was a brief whispered conference. "We want to do two hits together."

"Okay. Whatever." Tomás shrugged, taking one ticket from Amy and one ticket from the twins. They nestled their identical pink ruffled dresses side by side and gripped four small black hands around the bat. "Hey, I've only got one blindfold. Someone got another handkerchief?"

An elderly man in a black cassock stepped out of the shade to proffer his. Tomás tied a kerchief gently around the first twin's eyes and then the other. He tried to herd them in a circle but soon tired of the effort.

"You're next, Amy."

"I know, I know. This is really silly, but I'm, well, kind of excited."

The twins swung too high and hit the orange rope. Then they knocked off one of the dangling red rays, which had been damaged by a previous child's hit. They grinningly accepted their trophy, one twin holding each end of the ray.

"You're up."

"Everybody is watching," Amy said.

"Yeah. You've drawn quite a crowd," Lucia commented.

"It's embarrassing."

"Go on. You'll have fun." Lucia gave her back a gentle shove. Amy moved into place next to the piñata.

"You ever done this before?" Tomás asked.

"Never."

He grinned wickedly and tied the handkerchief in place. He turned her around and around until she was quite dizzy. Lucia handed him all her remaining tickets. Tomás silently made a circle with his finger and thumb as he mouthed "Okay." He turned Amy to face toward the piñata, its much-battered red crepe paper no longer hiding the newspaper beneath.

"Are you out of the way?" Amy asked Tomás.

"Yeah. Go for it," he replied.

Amy struck hard at thin air. She started to take the blindfold off.

"Hey, keep hitting," he said. "You've got four more swings."

Her second one also missed. The third one grazed a glancing blow off the side but no candy fell. Tomás signaled Beto, who lowered the piñata into Amy's fourth blow. The red star shattered, sprinkling wrapped candies over the ground. Squealing children ran from every direction.

"Quick, take the blindfold off or you'll miss all the candy," Lucia yelled.

Amy stripped off the kerchief and managed to snag a broken butterscotch. She unwrapped it and popped both pieces in her mouth. "I broke it. I did it," she said happily.

"You sure did. You really creamed it," Tomás said, handing her the bottom of the star with several candies still stuck in its newspaper. Beto was tying a new piñata to the rope.

"Santa Claus?" Lucia asked incredulously.

"Yeah. They're real cheap in May. So, you coming to the game next Saturday, Tía Lucia?"

"Maybe. We'll see." Lucia picked a peppermint out of the newspaper as she and Amy strolled away.

"Tía?" Amy asked, offering Lucia a candy.

"Courtesy aunt. We're cousins really, but when your cousin is a generation ahead of you, you usually call them aunt or uncle," Lucia explained.

"Gracías. That helps," Amy said, plucking the last candy out of the piñata before she deposited it in a trash can.

Lucia's beeper went off. A look of dismay crossed Amy's face. "It's probably nothing, Amy, but I do have to call in." Lucia strode away toward the main building, leaving Amy behind. When she returned, Amy was sitting at the bingo table, playing.

"I've got to go over to the jail. An informant has come forward in the Whittier case and an assistant DA and I have got to question her. Whittier was her pimp, so she probably does know something. I've got to be there in a half-hour, so I've got to run."

"Fine," Amy said, as the caller announced "B-7." "Bingo," yelled an excited woman, surrounded by teenage girls.

"Don't be that way, Amy. I can't help it. It's my job," Lucia pleaded.

"Yes, it's your job," said Amy flatly, pushing open all the numbers she had closed on the heavy cardboard bingo card.

"I've got to go."

"I'm staying. There are some things I want to get at the rummage sale. I'll walk home."

"Amy, I...we'll talk at dinner tonight." Amy did not turn around to watch Lucia's departure. Instead she stared at the branch decorated with dozens of small envelopes. The bingo winner selected one and showed it to the announcer, who led her to a large tin of imported cookies.

Lucia pushed open the heavy green door without a glance at the gilt outlining its carving. She chatted with the smiling young man in a dark grey suit as he led her to Amy's table. He pulled a ladder-back chair out from the table and seated Lucia.

After a moment of silence, she said, "I wasn't sure you'd be here."

"Don't be ridiculous. I was irritated at having our day spoiled. Come to think of it, I still am. But that's no reason to spoil our evening too. So did you find your murderer?"

Lucia covered her face with her hand and shook her head no. "Total bust," she said, dropping her hand. "Ms. Shawna Night was in serious need of a couple of hundred dollars, probably to feed her habit. She had been in Cancún with a wealthy customer, but she was sure we would pay her for 'background information.' It was a total wash. My guess is that Whittier got some major dealer or loan shark very angry. I doubt if we'll ever close that case. So have you decided on what you're having?" Lucia opened the tall green menu. "My, my. The first page is just drinks."

"I bet they come with little umbrellas. I'm having green tea and pock-marked ma's bean curd." She poured tea out of a squat white pot into a squat, white, handleless cup. Amy sipped her tea. "I thought about the duck, but I'm feeling like I need to be vegetarian for a while."

"Must have been the food at the fiesta. It would make a vegetarian out of anyone! Only the brownies were edible, and I'm always suspicious of brownies served by teenagers."

Amy laughed. "We were lovers for years before Laura told me about the first time she tried pot. Her older sister was given a baggie of it by a friend. Neither of them had any idea of how to roll a joint, so she and Laura dumped the baggie into a batch of spaghetti sauce. Her mother got very talkative during dinner and sang dirty songs while washing the dishes. Laura and her sister got the giggles."

"What about her father?" Lucia flipped back to the front of the menu, her attention more on the food than on Amy's story about her first lover.

"He went to sleep at the dinner table. You have to have met her family to appreciate the story. Her family is very straight, very Republican. Her father was a district court judge."

"Are you ready to order?" A high-school-aged woman with straight black hair and sparkling eyes stood behind the table.

"I'll have chicken in wonderful sauce," Lucia replied.

The waitress nodded while writing in Chinese on the order pad.

"And I'll have the Szechwan tofu." Both Amy and Lucia handed back the menus.

"Anything to drink?"

"A Tsing Tao beer, please," Lucia requested.

"I'll stick with green tea. It's lovely," Amy replied.

When dinner arrived, both chicken and tofu were coated in a satiny brown sauce. Bright green peas and vivid orange chunks of carrot were displayed on both plates. Lucia poured her beer carefully down the edge of the glass.

"Do you think it's the same dish with only a change in the protein?" Amy asked with an upraised eyebrow.

"I don't know. Maybe? Wait, I've got mushrooms in mine and you have water chestnuts in yours. Definitely different dishes."

Amy opened a long, thin box of carved wood beside her plate and took out a pair of chopsticks carved out of the same wood as the box.

"Those are beautiful," Lucia said. "How come they didn't come with my chicken? A special treat for vegetarians?"

"No. I brought them myself. Aunt Meg sent them to me from Beijing when she was there on a trip several years ago. I decided it was silly to leave them in a drawer, so I brought them along. They're mahogany." She handed the pair over to Lucia for examination. "I guess I remembered them because Aunt Meg called this afternoon. A friend of hers was murdered and she's very upset."

Lucia caressed the smooth wood, then positioned them for eating. "You've got to be kidding. What happened?"

"No one seems to be quite sure. Her family had arrived yesterday for a visit and found the woman dead in her apartment. At first they thought it was her heart, but she wasn't taking digitalis as a prescription and, at the autopsy, they found some in her stomach. So then they checked her apartment and her sugar bowl was full of digitalis. It's caused a tremendous stir in the retirement center, as you can imagine. Aunt Meg was quite beside herself."

Lucia finished chewing her chicken and returned the chopsticks to Amy. "It tastes wonderful, but it might just be the chopsticks. I wonder why the victim didn't taste the digitalis. Most medicine tastes terrible."

"I don't know. Maybe it's sweet like sugar." Amy carefully imprisoned a slick piece of tofu and popped it in her mouth. "Mmm. Maybe it is the chopsticks. This is even better than my recipe out of *Mrs. Chiang's Szechwan Cooking.*"

"Nope, not the special chopsticks. Must be the new chef because mine is great too." Lucia chased a pea around her plate before finally trapping it. "What else did Meg have to say?"

"I know this is stupid, but she seems to think some suspicion has fallen on her." Amy didn't attempt to disguise the note of worry in her voice. "Not very likely, is it?"

"Not unless she has motive, means, and opportunity, which seems very unlikely." Lucia pushed another pea into the pile of them she was creating on the left side of her plate. She appeared to be decorating the trees in the pattern on the plate. "I only met her when she came for Fiesta last spring, but she certainly didn't strike me as a mad poisoner."

"Don't tease about Aunt Meg, Lucia. She's the only decent relative I've got. If it hadn't been for her, I'd probably be in a mental institution." Amy stared for a moment at the dark wood of the chopsticks.

"Or in prison for killing your father," Lucia commented. "He certainly deserves it regardless of how a jury might react."

"Should incest be punishable by death, Detective Ramos?" Amy asked, pausing her tofu's journey at the end of the chopsticks.

"I'm coming to think so. But then, I'm not exactly objective. I want anyone who hurt you that badly for that long to be eliminated from the possibility of ever hurting you again." Lucia stared her conviction with grim firmness into Amy's eyes.

"You're wonderfully gallant, Lucia. But I don't need him dead anymore. Not since Aunt Meg maneuvered his approval for me to go to Rice. Houston is a long way from Chicago. Aunt Meg set me free."

"As she couldn't do for herself."

"No, not 'til after she graduated from law school. Not even during the Korean War. My father was too old for the draft and very nearsighted. Living with him must have been hell. My grandparents would never have believed anything like incest of their darling son, any more than my mother did of her perfect husband."

"Well, one thing you can say in favor of killing incest perpetrators is that they'll never do it again," Lucia commented.

"True, but the same could be said of virtually any crime, my bloodthirsty lover." Reassured by Lucia's vehemence, Amy began eating with vigor. "This is really quite a good tofu. I can't believe your chicken is as wonderful."

"It's great. Want a taste?"

"Sure, a mushroom, if you please. Would you like to try the tofu?" Amy lifted a square to Lucia's nodding head as Lucia maneuvered a mushroom cap toward Amy's open mouth.

"They're different sauces!" Amy exclaimed. "I think yours has bean paste."

"Please, don't tell me the ingredients. I don't want to know what's in Chinese food," Lucia said after washing some of the spicy residue of tofu down with her beer. "Yolanda and I went to San Francisco one summer. We wanted to see the gay Mecca. We didn't meet any gays because we had no idea where to look for them, other than softball games. It was before we knew about *Places of Interest to Women*, so we ended up in Chinatown mostly and had a great time anyway. There was this dim sum place we went to for lunch. We had no idea what we were eating. I had this small bowl of stew that was great, so I asked the waitress what it was. She didn't speak a lot of English, but she finally figured out what I was asking. 'Innards,' she said, pointing to her stomach. I guess I turned kind of green. Yolanda dumped what was left onto her plate and identified everything. Aorta, lungs, heart, thymus. I don't mind a great bowl of menudo, but this was too much even for me. I've never asked what was in a Chinese dish since. If it tastes fine that's all I care about." Lucia set to the remains of her dinner with a relish that confirmed her words.

"You don't talk about Yolanda much. Tell me about her."

"I've told you about her—how we met, how scared we were that anyone would know we were lovers, how she died. What else is there?"

"I don't know. I don't have an image of a real person. I have pictures in my mind like the ones in your album. She was very beautiful. But nothing moves. I want her to be real. Tell me something that will make her real. An idiosyncrasy."

Lucia looked puzzled. She popped a piece of carrot in her mouth and chewed it slowly. "It was funny. She never thought she was beautiful. 'My hips are too big; my breasts are too small,' she would always say. We were taking Art Appreciation and I saw slides of the Venus de Milo. They showed us about six different angles. I passed her a note, 'Whose body does that statue remind you of?' She was blushing. Even though the room was sort of dark I could tell. It was her body almost exactly. I guess it's my fate to fall in love with women who can't look in a mirror and see their own beauty. You blush just like my Yolanda did."

"You're just trying to distract me. I certainly don't look like the Venus de Milo."

"Nope, you're more Ruben's style."

"Back to Yolanda. What sorts of things made her sad?"

"She'd sorrow over the death of a child even if she didn't know him."

". . . or her."

"Or her. She had a cousin who died a couple of weeks after he was born, a staph infection, I think. Then her own brother died of TB like my mama. She took it very personally. That's why she wanted to be a microbiologist. She wanted to understand why these children died. She wanted to stop the deaths of other children. Perhaps because she knew she wouldn't have any of her own."

"She could have, though. Lots of lesbians have babies through artificial insemination."

"No. There was a malformation in her uterus. She couldn't carry a child."

"Then, you."

"I don't want a baby. I didn't then. I don't now."

"But you are so wonderful with children."

"I love being a tía, but I don't want to be a mother any more than I wanted to be a dentist."

"How come?"

"Scraping tartar off teeth and drilling holes in enamel just doesn't make my day." Lucia threw both hands in the air and shrugged. "Just weird that way, I guess."

"Okay. Okay. It was a stupid question. I take it back."

MONDAY

The insistent ringing of a phone woke Lucia out of a deep sleep. She stumbled out of bed and into her small living room. "If this is an obscene phone call, I will go to a bruja and have a curse put on you," she yelled at the still-ringing phone. She turned on the desk lamp and answered her old-fashioned black rotary dial phone. "Ramos residence, may I help you?"

"Lucia," Amy's voice sounded frantic. "They've arrested her. We've got to help."

"Who, Amy? Who've they arrested? What are you talking about?" Lucia asked groggily.

"Aunt Meg. They think she poisoned her friend. I don't know what to do. Please help. I don't know where to start."

"Did she call you?"

"No, a friend of hers named...just a minute, I wrote it down somewhere. Yes, here it is—Ruby Anne Sewell. She said the sheriff just left."

"Sheriff, that's too bad," Lucia commented, taking the phone over to her couch.

"What's wrong? Why is that bad?" Amy asked in a panic.

"Well, most of the rural ones I've had to deal with weren't very professional. They're more worried about re-election than justice for the most part."

"But why would he arrest Aunt Meg? I don't understand."

"I don't either," Lucia said. "Let me put some clothes on

and come over. In the meantime see if you can find out where she was taken. Oh, and make me a big pot of coffee. I'm going to need it."

All the way to Amy's, Lucia mulled the news over in her mind. What motive could gentle, classy Meg have for murdering an old lady? Money? Meg appeared to be independently wealthy. Was she being blackmailed? For what? Being an incest survivor? Being a lesbian? Was she a lesbian? Amy wasn't even sure. Was Meg a closet gambler, coke head, embezzler? It all seemed too unlikely. Did Meg have a heart problem? If not, where could she get digitalis? How could she have put it in someone's sugar bowl? Did she spend a lot of time in the victim's kitchen? Were they lovers? Could jealousy be a motive? The questions were endless. The simplest answer was that Meg was innocent. And the simplest answer was most often the right answer.

Amy hung up dissatisfied. Somehow she had expected Lucia to solve everything. "How unrealistic and unfair," she chided herself. She took a deep breath and held it for a moment before letting it go. Calmness was essential. She called her aunt's phone number in Mt. Vernon, Alabama. After twelve rings, she gave up. Next, she called Ruby Sewell back. The phone was answered on the second ring.

"Ms. Sewell, this is Amy Traeger, Meg Traeger's niece. We spoke a few moments ago. Can you tell me where my aunt was taken?"

"Why, I suppose over to the county jail. I believe it's probably at the courthouse over in Citronelle. It's a brand new county with a new courthouse. I had to go over there to get my driver's license. Everyone said it would be much faster than Mobile. Tensaw County Courthouse, Citronelle, Alabama. Is there anything else I can do, dear? Do you want me to drive over to the jail? She asked me not to get involved, but I'm so worried about Maggie. It's all quite dreadful." Deep concern was apparent in the tenor voice at the other end of the line.

"Thank you. I'm not sure it would help. Can I call you back if I think of something that needs to be done before morning?" Amy asked, pacing back and forth with her phone.

"Anything. Your aunt and I are very close friends. I would do absolutely anything to help. You just call, honey. Maggie will be so relieved that you're coming."

Amy spent the next half hour calling every airline in the phone book for schedules to Mobile. She made reservations for two on a flight through Dallas that would arrive at 2:30 the next afternoon. She booked a rental car at the Mobile airport. Lucia's knock interrupted her giving her credit card number to the rental agency. She hurried to open the door.

"Come in. I'm on the phone making a car reservation."

"Wouldn't it be faster to fly?" Lucia asked.

"This is no time for teasing, sweetheart," Amy said, going back to the phone to finish her call.

"I wasn't teasing," Lucia thought. She sat on the leather couch and yawned. She looked around for something to make notes on. Then she noticed the steno pad that Amy carried. That would do.

"First, we need a good lawyer," Lucia said. "A criminal lawyer."

"In Alabama, probably Mobile," Amy said. "Too bad I don't know any criminals in Mobile. Where are they when you need them?" Amy began to giggle, then she burst into sobs. Lucia pulled her onto the couch and held her while she wept. "I can't believe this is happening. I feel so helpless," she cried.

"It's okay, niña. We'll get this straightened out." Lucia

patted Amy's short, honey-brown curls. "There are lots of things we can do. We're not helpless. Don't worry, we'll clear your Aunt Meg." Gradually the sobbing stopped. Amy wiped away the tears streaked across her soft cheeks and wide lips.

"She needs a good lawyer most," she said. "I'm not sure how to go about finding one in another state. I don't think just calling the Bar Association is the best idea." Lucia took the notebook and pen out of Amy's hands.

"Let's write down the name of every lawyer we can think of. Looking at the list may give us some ideas of where to start." Two dozen names later they were out of ideas.

Amy looked at her phases-of-the-moon wristwatch. "Two a.m. I guess it's too early to call anyone. We don't want to make them mad."

"What do we do now?"

"Where's that coffee?"

"Oh, I forgot."

"Let's start a pot and think this through. After all, there's not much we can do until morning. That's why police pick people up after working hours. It not only intimidates them to pick them up in the middle of the night, it also cuts them off from support. Not many people have a lawyer on retainer who'll come down and deal with the police at 2 a.m."

"So you've done this sort of thing to suspects." Amy did not attempt to hide the disapproval in her voice.

"Yes, and sometimes it works. Remember, Amy, most of the people I arrest are guilty. They've killed someone and will likely kill someone else if we don't stop them. I assure you, I have never dragged some innocent old lady out of her bed to try to terrorize her into a false confession. Cross my heart." Lucia paused, then plunged into her next line of thinking. "What if Meg isn't innocent? We need to consider that possibility. Police don't arrest people on a whim even in the wilds of Alabama. They must have some evidence to link her to the crime."

"Impossible."

"Amy, we're not going to help your aunt by keeping our eyes or our minds closed. It's a possibility, no matter how remote, that we need to consider."

"If she didn't murder her brother during all those years he was raping her and me, she could not kill anyone, any time, for any reason. Period."

"Are you talking about Meg or Amy?"

"Don't try psychobabble on a shrink, Lucia. It doesn't work. I am talking about my aunt and you know it."

"Amy, you yourself said that you don't know your aunt Meg that well. You aren't even sure she is a lesbian. There are lots of things about her you don't know. Maybe someone she loves was endangered by the victim. There might be lots of explanations. We can't know for sure."

"I do."

"Okay. Can we agree to disagree about this? Is it okay for me to keep my opinion open or will that seem like a betrayal to you?" Lucia spoke with over a ycar's experience in negotiating with Amy.

Amy took several minutes to consider. "It's okay, but I don't want to discuss the possibility. Please keep it to yourself. It won't make me crazy then, and I suppose it's only sensible. So, what do we do now?"

"We could make that pot of coffee. And I suppose we could call the jail and find out her status. My guess is she hasn't been charged yet. The police have twenty-four hours they can hold someone without letting them make a call or charging them. We should probably find out about the DA's office. They call the shots from here on out. Who knows? They may refuse to charge her."

Amy brought the remote phone from the kitchen wall over to the table. Lucia filled the coffeepot. She sat back down at the table and stared at the Laurel Burch cats design on the mugs. She revived a bit as the scent of the coffee filled the kitchen, while Amy tried different names for the jail to get the phone number. "What's the name of the county?" Lucia whispered.

"Tensaw," Amy replied.

Lucia wrote "Tensaw County Correctional Facility" on the steno pad and showed it to Amy.

"It worked," Amy said, writing the phone number below its title. "How did you know?"

"The current fad in names. A jail is a jail, but some people believe you can get more funding if you change its title in the budget request."

"Now what do I ask? I don't even know the right questions."

"Depends on whether this is a big facility or a small one. If it's big, you just ask if she's been entered on the books as being in custody. That's all they're going to tell you. If it's small, they might even let you talk to her. Worth a try."

Amy called the number and was answered by a yawning female voice, "Whatcha want?"

"I'd like to know if you have Margaret Traeger in custody?"

"Yeah."

"Could I talk to her?"

"Naw. She's asleep. Call back in the morning." The line went dead.

"What did they say?" Lucia asked.

"It was a woman. She said Meg was sleeping and to call back." Amy sounded bemused.

"She probably meant that she was sleeping." Lucia yawned. "Which isn't a bad idea. There's not much more we can do until business hours. Alabama is on Central Time, same as we are. So...." She swallowed a last gulp of the decaf.

"I don't think I can sleep. Why don't you take my bed and I'll sit around and obsess."

"Great idea. Oh, what about air reservations? I presume you're going out to Alabama tomorrow."

"I've already made them...for two."

"Two? You going to take a lawyer with you from here?"

"I'd rather take a homicide detective, if she can see her way clear to accompany me. Will you help me, Lucia? I really need you," Amy pleaded.

"I don't know, Amy. I'd have to get off work. I don't know if I can."

"In one year you have taken off two long weekends. That's a grand total of two days of vacation used. I'm sure you're due some time off."

"But you have to schedule vacation months ahead."

"Do you not want to come with me?"

"Sure, I want to come and help. I just don't know if I can swing it."

"Personal leave, family emergency. There must be provisions for things like that."

"Yes, there are. I'll try, Amy. I'll try." The rest of her words were lost in a yawn.

Amy smiled as she turned around. Lucia stood there naked, toweling off her short black hair with a maroon towel. "Magnífico. You are a distraction from my troubles, Lucia Ramos," she said.

"Hey, your español está muy bueno, querida." Lucia lassoed her with the towel and pulled her close for a long deep kiss. "Mmm, good morning. Any of that coffee left? Made any headway on a lawyer? Do you have another bar of soap? I used up the last of yours. Just tell me where it is. I'll get it."

Amy ran her palms firmly up and down Lucia's smooth brown back, feeling the strength of her muscles. "You'd better get dressed before I lose track of my mission. Tom from upstairs is tracking down a judge from Mobile, and I left a message on about ten answering machines and with one receptionist. Nada más. I'll make your coffee. Want some cocoa in it?" Lucia nodded as Amy continued without pause. "Soap is behind the towels on the third shelf of the linen closet." Lucia raised an eyebrow. "I know it's odd, but how often does one person need to get out a fresh bar of soap? Every month? I use the sheets every week. Why am I explaining? Go, get dressed." She kissed Lucia on the ear and gave her a gentle shove.

"Okay, but soften that 'd' in nada. Make it a little closer to a 'th.' It'll sound more authentic."

"It's 7:40 in the morning and she's giving me language lessons," Amy said to Lucia's retreating back.

"Okay, Ramos. Let's cut to the heart of it. You want time off to help this shrink friend of yours spring her aunt on a murder charge, right?" Lieutenant Reynolds waved the chewed end of his unlit cigar in Lucia's direction.

"Yes, sir," Lucia said. "That about covers it." She shifted uncomfortably in the army surplus chair in front of Reynolds' desk, wondering if she should have worn a skirt.

"Not smart, Ramos, getting involved in some other department's case. They're gonna resent the hell out of it. I don't want any complaints coming back to this department. Keep your nose clean." He pushed his chair back and propped his feet on the desk.

"So I can have leave?" Lucia asked, amazed at the ease with which her request had been granted.

"Sure. You've got plenty of vacation time. All your cases are caught up, according to Graciella. No court dates. No one else out. Why not?" He stuck the cigar back in his mouth, then took it out again. "Just keep in mind, Ramos, maybe the old lady did it. What then?"

"I don't know, Lieutenant. That could be a problem. But if I find evidence, I turn it over. Doesn't matter who it incriminates." Lucia knew in her heart that she would, in fact, do exactly that. And she knew that Amy would never forgive her if she incriminated Meg.

"You're a good cop, Ramos. Don't let friendship mess that up. After all, most poisoners are women. That's where you look first."

"Thanks for the advice, Lieutenant Reynolds. And for the time off." Lucia rose out of the chair.

"Good luck, Ramos, and keep out of the way of the local department, right?"

"Right." Lucia turned and left the cubicle of an office. She stopped at Graciella's desk on her way out. She smiled into Graciella's twinkling brown eyes. "So, thanks for telling Reynolds I was caught up on my paperwork."

"Pretty much, you are. I don't care if anyone ever turns in a 10/42 ever again. It's a stupid report and the DA has no right to ask for it. 'A one-page summary of all current cases to facilitate communication,' indeed. Nothing but a time saver for his prima donnas. Let 'em read the regular report like everybody else, I say," Graciella growled in mock fury. She shook her waist-length black hair and bared her teeth. "As if we didn't kill enough trees already with bureaucratic stupidity."

"Anyway, thanks. Eric is taking anything that comes up on my cases."

"He should. You covered for him for a month while his kid was in the hospital. So I hear you're going on a busman's holiday. First real time off in two years and you're going to work a case in Alabama! You're nuts, Lucia. Get a life. Go to Vegas or Hawaii. If you want to see how another department works, check out San Francisco or Montreal. But Alabama, for god's sake. I don't get it. You got a strange idea of a holiday, Lucia."

"I owe Amy Traeger. She really broke the Freeman case.

This is a debt. I pay my debts. Besides, Graciella, she's a good friend," Lucia added.

"Get out of here, Lucia. You're nuts, but you're an honorable woman. Go pay your debt. You've got to be back next Monday at 7 a.m. sharp, though, debts paid or not." She waved Lucia away with a sheaf of papers. "Good luck, Officer Ramos, and be careful. You're most likely to get hurt when you let your guard down."

Her phone was ringing as she entered her little house. She rushed to pick it up before it quit. She didn't want to miss Amy if that's who it was.

"Good morning, Lucia Ramos. This is Freddie Christian. My lawyer, Juanita Morales, just called and told me you were in need of some help."

Lucia shook her head. Freddie Christian's lovely tenor was the last voice she expected to hear on her phone. "Whatever happened to client confidentiality?" she asked, bemused.

"Juanita works only for me. You should have remembered that when you called her. Besides, Juanita is sending the bill to me, not your friend Dr. Traeger. Therefore I am the client and need to know everything. I have a large debt to you, Lucia, which you've never allowed me to pay." Freddie's whisky tenor held a faint and unusual note of pleading.

"Ms. Christian, it was my job to arrest your lover's murderer. You paid me with your tax money. Besides, I am more than compensated by your very generous donation of her estate to the Cuero Safe House. It's made a tremendous difference in the lives of those kids. That's it. Debt over."

"Nonsense. I would have given the money away. It was blood money. You simply were of assistance in my decision."

"As you were, in getting rid of a bad cop, which also put me in your debt," Lucia sparred.

"Piffle. I would have turned him in for selling me information in any case. Citizens cannot afford to tolerate any corruption in the police force," Freddie dismissed her cooperation in the firing of the Evidence Room duty officer.

"Then quit trying to corrupt me, Freddie," Lucia ordered in an exasperated tone. "I have about three minutes to pack and get out of here. I don't have time for this."

"Officer Ramos, I am not going to corrupt you with the offer of a few names of possible allies in southern Alabama. I suspect you don't know a soul there. So if you are in such a tremendous rush I suggest you drop your demurrals and take notes. First, Zena Beth Grey..."

"The lesbian writer?" Lucia interrupted while she searched her desk drawer for a pen.

"Of course. She lives in Mt. Blanchard, a couple of hours northeast of Mt. Vernon. I thought she might have police contacts since she's writing murder mysteries, or rather, her cat is. Her phone is 855-9932. The next name is Betty Ann McCaran at 627-7115 in Mobile. She runs the national Junior Miss competition and knows everybody who is anybody. The last name Helen Frances. She's the CEO for Mobile Memorial Hospital. Her home phone is 822–6075. You've probably heard of her lover, Sandra Coolidge, the writer."

"My god, is Sandra Coolidge a lesbian?" Lucia asked.

"No time for gossip, Officer Ramos. I understand you have a plane to catch. I'll call these friends to prepare them for your possible need for assistance. Bueno suerte y adios." The line went dead.

"Freddie Christian's 'Sapphic circle' is wide, indeed," Lucia mused as she emptied her underwear drawer into her suitcase. "Who would have thought that a rich half-Mexican cantaloupe grower from Freer, Texas, would know both Zena Beth Grey and Sandra Coolidge's lover." Lucia broke off that line of thought to contemplate T-shirts. In went her lavender moon tree design with the rhinestones and her current favorite, the rattlesnake from Big Bend. Next went a pair of black jeans. She turned to her closet and took out three sets of work clothes, the beige pantsuit with the ice blue blouse, the teal slacks and matching top, and finally, just in case, the black skirt with jacket and white blouse. She tossed in every pair of clean pantyhose she could find, wincing at the thought of wearing them in the humid heat of the Gulf coast.

Next was the medicine chest. She picked the blue toothbrush with sparkles in the plastic that Amy had given her last month and put it in the zip-lock baggie with a tube of Crest. These were followed by deodorant, Cachet perfume, aspirin, mascara, and two shades of lip gloss. She hesitated at the bottle of Mega-stress B vitamins that Tía Luz insisted were important to her health, then shrugged and tossed it in. "Given the givens, it couldn't hurt," she thought, zipping the top of the baggie. Everything went in the old green Samsonite bag. In her leather carry-on from Laredo she put her shampoo and cream rinse, her tape recorder, two notebooks, a handful of Bic pens, and her half-read copy of Silko's *Almanac of the Dead* which she had picked up at Textures, the women's bookstore on McCullough. She looked around wondering what she had forgotten. "Okay, well," she thought, "I'm sure they have stores in Mt. Vernon."

Lucia flew out the door and dumped the bags in the back seat of her Sentra. She was sorely tempted to speed to the airport. "Keep your nose clean," she thought. "Reynolds won't be impressed if you get caught in an impropriety before you even get outside the city limits." She did, however, keep her speed about seven miles above the speed limit.

"Did you find a lawyer?" Lucia said after settling in the

wide seat next to Amy.

"Yes. He's supposed to be the best in the southern part of Alabama, according to Tom's friend, the judge. His name is Andrew Byrd. We have an appointment with him at three-thirty this afternoon." She tried to smother a huge yawn.

"Why don't you try to nap, Amy? Then you'll be rested when we get there," Lucia urged.

Amy nodded. She wedged a small pillow between her head and the window and closed her eyes. She slept through most of the flight to Mobile while Lucia flirted with the flight attendant. The novelty of flying first class also entertained Lucia.

When they checked in at the rental agency's reservation desk, everything went smoothly. Amy listed both herself and Lucia as drivers, then they walked outside to the baby blue Skylark that was waiting for them. Amy elected to drive.

As soon as they were on the interstate, she began to talk about Meg's imprisonment.

"I can't believe my aunt is in jail, Lucia. This all seems like a nightmarc I can't wake up from."

"At lcast it's new, Amy. It'll probably be clean. That'll help. Most prisoners complain of boredom more than anything else."

"Well, she won't have time to be bored. We'll get her out on bail."

"I hope so, Amy, but don't count on it."

"What do you mean? Even guilty people get bail. Aunt Meg isn't even guilty. Of course she'll get bail." Amy tried to sound confident.

"Well, the judge and the grand jury may not believe that she's innocent. If the grand jury brings in an indictment—I mean if there's a grand jury, I don't know how it works in Alabama—the judge may or may not feel bail is appropriate. Poisoning is virtually always premeditated, and Meg didn't grow up in the community she'll be tried in." Lucia tried to pat Amy's hand, which was clenched around the steering wheel.

"I can't believe that a grand jury would indict Aunt Meg for murder." Amy's usually generous lips were drawn into a tight hard line.

"You can't predict what juries will do, Amy. Most of them try very hard to do the best job they know how, but who can guess what they'll believe is best? Not me. I've testified in front of a hundred different juries and they still surprise me," Lucia said, shaking her head. She gave up trying to reason with Amy and the rest of the drive was silent.

Amy pulled into the parking garage that occupied the second floor of the Stone Tower office complex. She found a parking space near the elevator. The brief trip to the eleventh floor was accompanied by classical music emitting from a speaker in the ceiling.

The furnishings in Byrd's office matched the expensive location. Oriental rosewood chests and tables were interspersed by four comfortable chairs upholstered in cream-colored brocade. The pattern was perfectly set off by the grey in the carpeting. On one large, metal-banded chest a candle was lit inside a grey-green porcelain lantern. The faint odor of sandlewood permeated the room.

"You must be Amy Traeger. I'm Rosalyn Eisenberg, Mr. Byrd's assistant." An attractive woman in her early sixties rose from behind the desk and extended her hand for a firm handshake. "You're a tad early, so why don't we have a cup of tea or some other refreshment?" She ushered them through a side door as Amy introduced Lucia.

"How wonderful that you don't have to endure this ordeal alone. This is a great kindness you are doing, Ms.

Ramos. A criminal proceeding is often a time of very great stress for people, don't you find, Ms. Ramos?"

Lucia nodded her agreement.

"Perhaps something hot to drink will settle your nerves. We have several types of Oriental teas. I'm very partial to our Japanese green tea."

"The green would be lovely," Amy murmured. "Was it you I spoke with on the phone? The directions were excellent."

Lucia sat quietly sipping her tea out of a tiny fragile cup in grey green porcelain and listening to Amy and Rosalyn murmur polite conversation to each other. The phone never rang to distract them. After several minutes Rosalyn graciously excused herself and returned to her duties in the outer office. Lucia checked her watch. It was two minutes until their appointment time.

"This is quite an operation," she commented. "It feels more like the office of a bank president than a criminal lawyer."

"I find it very reassuring," Amy said. "Some of the criminal lawyers I've met seemed more at home inside the bars than out."

"Yeah, and these days a lot of bank presidents belong behind bars."

There was a rap at the door and a red-headed man in his late thirties stuck his head through. "Amy Traeger?" he inquired.

"Yes, and you are..."

"Andrew Byrd. Roz told me you brought an associate with you." He bustled into the room and settled behind the desk. He removed a yellow pad and a pen from the center drawer. "I understand you're a homicide detective, Ms. Ramos. Nothing better on the case than someone with the family who understands police procedure. It clears up many misunderstandings before they occur. I don't have to spend so much time explaining what I can't do. I did call the DA's office in Tensaw County. No charges have been filed. She does not have an attorney of record. I charge $250 an hour for my personal time. Research is billed at $75 an hour. Would you like me to explain what billable time includes or are you familiar with the concept?" He made a note on his pad.

"I understand. Will you take on my aunt's defense?"

"On two conditions. First, that I receive a $10,000 retainer and second, that my retention is agreeable to the defendant. Regardless, this meeting will be billed at regular rates whether I am retained or not."

"Certainly," Amy assented and began to write him a check.

"What do you know about the case?" he asked.

"Almost nothing. I received a call from Aunt Meg late Sunday afternoon. She was very distressed because a woman she played bridge with was apparently poisoned with digitalis. My aunt lives in a retirement home in Mt. Vernon called Heritage House. She's lived there for about a year. I've visited her twice and met several of her friends but not the woman who died. I have no idea who might have killed the victim. Frankly, I don't even remember her name. Apparently, someone put digitalis in her sugar bowl and she died after eating it at breakfast on Saturday.

"Her family didn't believe that she had a heart attack and demanded an autopsy," Amy continued. "When digitalis showed up, the sheriff decided it was murder since the victim didn't have a prescription for it. They checked what she had been eating and found it in the sugar. I have no idea why they arrested my aunt for the murder."

"Very well," Byrd said. "We'll know soon enough. So, do you have anything to add, Ms. Ramos?"

"No, except...I am a trained homicide investigator, but I have no jurisdiction in this case."

"Well, let us analyze the problem," Byrd said somewhat pompously. "We have a trained investigator, but that investigator has no right to investigate. Hm. Perhaps if you could get a private investigator's license...no, that could take months." He tapped his mahogany-clad pen against his mahogany desktop.

"I only have six days of leave left," Lucia mentioned.

"So, what else? Expert witness? Certainly. Consultant to examine evidence, part of our right of discovery. That's pushing it pretty far...it's worth a try."

"Is there any way I can visit Aunt Meg?" Amy asked. "Will they let me in?"

"Perhaps. I'll get my people working on it. Why don't you get settled and give me a call to let me know how to contact you."

"We'll be staying in her apartment at Heritage House," Lucia said.

"Excellent," he said. "I'll set my people to work on the case. Here is my private line. I'm generally in the office until 7 p.m. or so. I come in about 10 a.m. when I don't have to be in court. Call me with any information you feel might be useful. Good day." He walked abruptly from the officc.

"I guess they don't teach social skills in law school," Lucia commented.

"Apparently not. Since we are obviously dismissed, I guess we should leave."

The rental car wasn't cool, but the shade inside the parking garage kept it more or less the same temperature as the hot muggy air. The streets of Mobile quickly gave way to countryside. Flat fields spread behind the thick fence-row of trees. Some of the fields were planted in pine trees in varying stages of young growth. An occasional pump jack was bobbing up and down like a demented praying mantis, but most of the oil well pumpers were motionless.

There was a general aura of decay to the drive. Many of the old farmhouses were long abandoned. Some had collapsed into a pile of wood.

Several oil tank trucks sped past them heading to Mobile. "Did you notice the sign on that last truck? Groendyke. I like that name," Lucia commented.

"Nice," Amy agreed. "Do you think we can figure out who killed the victim?"

"I don't know. Lieutenant Reynolds said that most poisoners are women and that agrees with the studies I've read. That's a beginning."

"I think most women are hesitant to put themselves at risk, even for murder. Poison is safer for the murderer," Amy commented.

"And most men kill out of rage, on some sort of power trip. I suspect they like watching the victim die."

"That's gruesome, but you're probably right," Amy said. "It can't be too much farther to Citronelle."

"Just a couple of miles. We should be seeing the outskirts soon."

"Except for the trees, we might see it now." Amy gestured at the dense stand of pine they were driving through. "It reminds me of Big Piney. Laura and I used to go there from Houston for the weekends."

"There's nothing like this in southern Texas. Just mesquite scrub, not what you'd call a real forest," Lucia replied, slowing down for the forty-five miles per hour sign. The town of Citronelle looked out of place in the South. The houses were tall with steep-pitched roofs. Most were constructed out of white clapboard except for an occasional brick house. Both sides of the street were lined with large trees until they reached the commercial section. Lucia pulled up to a filling station and asked directions for the courthouse.

"Just keep on going up Main Street. You'll hit it in about a half mile." He continued speaking past Lucia's nod.

"It's where the old Tabor school used to be. School was built in the fifties when they hit oil here." He made oil into a three-syllable word. "Had asbestos all over it. Had to be torn down. They put this big plastic bubble over it like something out of a *Star Wars* movie." Lucia interrupted him with her thanks and drove off before he could begin to chat again.

The new courthouse was easy to recognize. It was by far the largest building they had yet seen in Citronelle. The four-story windowless monolith of white marble was dazzling in the summer sun and totally dwarfed the two-story brick dress shop next to it. They parked in a visitors' space. The hot pavement sank beneath their footsteps.

"Did you crack your window?" Lucia asked.

"Absolutely. This heat is unreal. I feel like I'm in a bowl of soup."

"Yeah. Hidalgo is like this in the summer. Heat and humidity. Thank heaven San Antonio is on the Edwards Plateau." Lucia tried the glass door from the parking lot. It was locked. When she looked inside she didn't see anyone about to open it. "I guess we'll have to go all the way around to the front."

"I'm drenched now. I think I should have worn a swimsuit instead of a business suit," Amy commented.

"You look great in execu-drag. At least your deodorant didn't fail."

"My god, Ramos, you're right. The only dry parts of my body are my armpits. Where do you think the jail is?" she asked as they walked in the front door together. A blast of cool air chilled them.

"Probably the top floor or the basement for security. It makes it just that much harder to escape. Since there aren't any windows, I'd bet on the top floor. If there were windows, I'd bet on the important offices being up there." She checked the directory next to the banks of elevators.

"Bingo! Top floor. I guess we just ride up and see what happens."

The wood-toned Formica doors of the elevator opened into a hallway with a closed door on either end. Lucia led the way to the one with a large sign on it:

Tensaw County Correctional Facility
Visiting Hours Daily from 4-6 p.m.
Ring for Entrance

"I can tell it's new," Lucia commented as she rang the bell.

"How?" Amy whispered.

"Pretty soon there'll be a second sign listing all the prohibited items that can't be brought in." Lucia fell silent as they waited for the door to open. After several minutes she rang again. A disheveled, heavy-set matron in an unflattering brown uniform stood behind the opening door.

"Sorry, I thought you was Darrel Richard's wife. She always shows up on Monday about this time. She's a mean one, so I don't hurry much for her. Who'ya here to see?" She smiled a hearty grin at them. "I bet I know. I bet you're here to see that old lady that poisoned her bridge partner. You're her daughters, right? I'm Brenda Sullivan, I run this here jail. Pleased to meet you." The front door slid closed before she gestured to the control booth operator to open the next door, which was heavy metal with barred windows. "You'll have to visit in her cell. She's in solitary until the arraignment. You'll have to leave your purses and everything here. I'll watch them. Don't worry. They wouldn't be safer in Fort Knox."

"May I take my notebook and a pen in?" Lucia asked.

"Let me check." Officer Sullivan checked a list posted near the glass double doors marked "Visitors." "Yeah, that'd be okay. Just put that other stuff on my desk and follow me." She gestured again for the door operator to release the opposite door and stepped through as it swung open.

Amy took a deep breath and walked through.

"Oops, I forgot to have you sign in. Oh, well, you can just do it when you sign out. Hurry up now, that darn thing doesn't stay open too long." She motioned Lucia to hurry. "I'm real glad you girls are here. Your mom is real down. Say, you got different dads? You sure don't look much like sisters." Amy nodded wordlessly as the matron signaled the release of the cell door.

Meg's brown and silver hair was hanging loose to her waist instead of pinned up in its usual bun. Her brown eyes, puffy from crying, lit with joy and relief as she recognized her niece. She threw open her arms and flew the few steps across the tiny cell, her navy jail uniform flapping loosely about her.

"Thank god! Oh, Amy, I prayed you'd come. Oh, dear, what am I to do? What am I to do?" she cried, fiercely holding Amy to her breast.

"I'll just let you girls alone. Be back in fifteen minutes. It's the rules." The jovial matron backed out the door and signaled it to be secured.

"It's all right, Aunt Meg. We're here, we're here," Amy said, stroking the crown of her head with one hand and holding the sobbing woman close with the other. "Lucia's come with me. We're going to get you out of here. It's going to be all right."

Meg Traeger pulled herself together and gently disengaged from her frantic embrace. She hugged Lucia with more reserve. "Thank you. I don't know how I can ever repay your kindness. I thought I was going insane. This is all so bizarre, Lucia. I just have no idea how to react. What am I to do?"

"There's not much you can do in here, Meg," Lucia replied. "We've found a good criminal lawyer named Andrew Byrd to take your case, and Amy and I will help him as much as we can. What you can do is tell us whatever you know. I hate to be abrupt, but we don't have much time and we have a lot to talk about." Lucia lowered herself onto the grey linoleum floor and opened her notebook.

"Oh, yes, of course. It's just that I'm starved for company. The evening matron is sweet, but she doesn't stay to talk. There aren't any windows and the light in the hall stays on all night. I can't sleep or eat or read or do anything but think. I felt like I was going mad," Meg said, slowly and carefully lowering herself to the floor.

"We're here to help. You'll be out soon. This place is designed for sensory deprivation. It's absolutely horrible." Amy sat also.

"It was designed for cheap security. And I don't know when you'll be out, Meg, but I hope it's very soon. Who is the victim and how do you know her?" Lucia slipped easily into her police investigator mode.

"Lorretta Millett. She's in my bridge club. My friend Ruby..."

"She's the one who called us," Amy interjected.

"She's wonderful. I hoped she would do that...."

"Tell us about the bridge club." Lucia pulled the conversation back on track.

"Ruby's friend, Minerva, asked us to join when a couple of spots opened up. We met every Friday at a different apartment to play duplicate bridge. We played at Lorretta's this last Friday. She died Saturday at the very same table where we played bridge. We didn't have the usual two tables because Sylvia and Edith were away on a cruise." Meg shifted on the hard floor trying to get comfortable.

"So there were at least four other women with access to the sugar bowl on Friday," Lucia said.

"Shaker. It was a blue glass cinnamon-sugar shaker that the digitalis was in."

"How do you know that?" Amy asked, surprised.

"Ruby heard it from one of the girls in the office who's a

cousin to the sheriff. Everybody at Heritage House was talking about it."

"Was she well liked? The victim, I mean?" Lucia asked, catching up on her notes.

"Well, I hate to speak badly of the dead, but no, she wasn't a warm person. She was always, well, searching for an advantage to have over others." Meg tried to knot her hair up in a twist, but it fell loose.

"She liked to be in control?" Amy asked.

"You could say that, dear, and it would be a fair assessment."

"Did everyone who played bridge that day have access to the sugar shaker?" Lucia inserted.

"Yes, it was on the kitchen counter. We were all in and out getting water or tea or something. I didn't pay much attention."

"Who else was at the bridge game besides you and Lorretta Millett? Ruby?"

"Yes, and Minerva. And Helen Carlisle and Dorothy Hoffman."

"Tell me about them, please." Lucia was writing furiously.

"Helen is rather odd. She is always smiling, but I don't think she's a very happy person. She is very active in the Presbyterian church. That's how she picked Heritage House. It's owned by five major churches in Mobile. Baptist, Methodist, Episcopalian, Lutheran, and Presbyterian. The director, Sam Pettigrew, is an ex-priest as well as an ex-banker."

"That seems odd among all these Protestant churches," Amy commented as she stroked Meg's hair into a semblance of order.

"Yes. I've never met an ex-priest before. He's quite a nice man. Very trustworthy."

"What about Dorothy Hoffman?" Lucia prodded.

"Oh, she has several children. Or is it two? I've not met

them. They don't seem to visit, but that isn't uncommon at Heritage House."

"What is she like?" Lucia asked.

"She's a very negative person. Other than that, she reminds me a good deal of the woman who owned the newspaper on that TV show with Ed Asner."

"The 'Mary Tyler Moore Show'?" Amy offered as she squirmed for a more comfortable position without jarring anyone else's limbs in the tiny cell. She finally draped her left elbow over the rim of the seatless toilet and leaned on it.

"No, the later one, set in California, I think."

"'Lou Grant'?" Amy tried again.

"Yes. Mrs. Somebody owned the paper."

"Pinchon?"

"Yes. I think that was how it was pronounced. My memory is just awful. I can't think of the word and it's so frustrating."

"Stress can do that. I wouldn't worry too much about it, Aunt Meg."

"So tell me about this Dorothy Hoffman," Lucia requested.

"I need to sit on the cot. This floor is too hard and cold. I hope you don't mind my being above you." She rose with some difficulty and sat on the edge of the cell's narrow bed. "Dorothy is very well-bred. When we have bridge at her apartment, she is always sure to send us little notes inviting us and has small hostess gifts like a tiny potted cactus or something. But she has nothing good to say about anything. If you say 'It's nice that today is a bit cooler,' she'll answer, 'But it's supposed to be much hotter tomorrow.' She loves to talk about people's faults. And now *I'm* sounding just like her." Meg shook her head.

"What about Minerva, Aunt Meg? Didn't I meet her during my last visit? I think her leg was in a cast," Amy mused.

"Yes, she broke her ankle in a fall down the stairs. She's

much better now, not even using a cane. Heavens, I don't know what to say about Minerva. She's solid as a rock. But sad. She seems to miss her roommate a great deal. They had lived together for almost fifty years. But at our age death begins to claim the people we love while the people we despise seem impervious to aging."

"Like my father," Amy commented.

"Yes, dear. That is who I was thinking of."

"What's Minerva's last name?" Lucia asked.

"Worthington. I'm sorry. I should have said that earlier."

"Was she close to Lorretta?" Lucia continued the interview.

"No, not at all. I believe that the bridge club was their primary connection. Both Minerva and Lorretta were very serious about bridge. Both played for Master's Points in tournaments in Mobile. None of the rest of us were quite as committed." Meg spread the cot's thin grey blanket over her legs.

"And Ruby. We need to know about Ruby Sewell," Amy said. "She's been very helpful."

"She's a very dear friend. She comes from New Mexico, where she was an editor of a small town newspaper. She grew up on her father's ranch. I know she didn't care for Lorretta, but she rarely spoke about her. That's Ruby's way. She'd rather keep quiet than to speak unkindly." Meg began to weep.

"I just can't be myself in these circumstances. I can't even put my hair up, I don't have any pins. If only they had arrested me during the day...."

"We'll see if we can't bring you a little supply of toiletries," Amy said. She moved into the space against the wall that Meg had vacated. "And a sweater. It's surprisingly cool in here."

"Please. Being disheveled makes me even more frantic."

Lucia thought for a moment, then asked, "Who might have wanted Lorretta dead?"

"Dorothy, I suppose. She was quite close to Earl Banks and he has also been seeing Lorretta. Dorothy has not taken it well."

"Who else?"

"I can't imagine."

"Who knew Ms. Millett? Did she have a maid, a hairdresser, someone who fixed her car? Perhaps a secretary? Who were her close friends?"

"I don't know who she was close to. She often sat at dinner with one of the bridge club or with the Hoskins who lived across the hall from her. When she wasn't dining with Earl, of course. She had the same maid we all did. Little Ruth Hankel. Such a sweet girl. And I'm fairly sure that Kay Newbolt did her hair. Lately I've seen her up at the office chatting with...oh, what is her name? I'm really not this forgetful, Amy. I do know her name." Meg shook her head in frustration.

"It's not important. We can just ask at the office, Meg," Lucia said. "Tell us about the last time you saw the victim. Was it at the bridge club?"

Meg shook her head no. She seemed reluctant to speak.

"You need to tell us about it, Aunt Meg. It's important." Amy looked at her aunt's sorrowing face.

"The last time I saw her she was very angry," Meg said.

"Try to remember exactly what happened," Lucia urged.

Meg sighed. "Memory is no longer my strongest point."

"Okay. Let's start with where it was."

"Her apartment. I went downstairs to ask her to reconsider." Meg's voice shook.

"Reconsider what?" Lucia probed.

"She had deduced my sexual preference. Or someone told her. I don't actually know how she found out. But she felt it was important to 'notify the authorities'. I presumed that meant talking with the director." Meg took a deep breath.

"What did she say when you asked her to reconsider?" Lucia prompted.

"She laughed. She said she didn't have time to worry about that. Then she said that what she was concerned about now involved fifty percent more people than my 'little problem' could touch. Then she started talking with percentages. I was so distraught that I didn't follow her."

"Please try to remember, Aunt Meg. It could be important," Amy broke in. Lucia shot her a warning glance. Amy was staring at Meg so intently that she missed it.

"I just don't recall, dear. I was trying so very hard to make Lorretta listen to me that I wasn't listening to her. That was really quite rude of me, but I was terrified. It's amazing to discover that one's manners are only a veneer quickly stripped away when inconvenient."

"Why did Lorretta think you were a lesbian?" Lucia tried to refocus the conversation.

Meg began a soft weeping. "I gave her a book last week, *Journal of a Solitude.* She seemed so very alone. I just thought it might help for her to read May Sarton. That book was such a resource for me when I lived alone. I wrote a sentiment on the fly leaf. I suppose I should tell you about it since it could be misinterpreted. I wrote, 'Please let these words and their sender into your heart.'"

"It sounds very sweet." Amy sounded puzzled.

"Yes, but I've been thinking about it a lot since I was arrested. I've certainly had time to think. A person with a suspicious turn of mind might believe that the word 'sender' referred to me rather than Miss Sarton, which was what I intended as I wrote it. If I was the sender referred to by the note, it could be interpreted as an effort at courtship, which is, of course, absurd. It could then be construed that I was an angry, jilted lover. Please tell me that my isolation has led to bizarre imaginings."

"I wish I could, Aunt Meg. But your conjectures strike me as quite possible." Amy moved to the cot so she could wrap her arms around Meg. "This is awful, Aunt Meg, but we've been through much worse."

"It's true, dear. We have. But this is so terribly public. I have always tried to keep my private life private." Meg dissolved completely into weeping, surrounded by Amy's arms. Amy held her until the matron came to tell them to leave.

Lucia held the keys out toward Amy. "Would you like to drive or should I do it?"

"Go ahead. I'm too distracted. Let's let it air a bit, though. It's got to be an oven inside."

Lucia nodded and opened both doors. "Cracking the windows can only do so much," she agreed. "I was glad you explained to the matron that we weren't Meg's daughters. She might have gotten mad if she'd heard it from someone else. And it doesn't pay to make jail officials mad at you. Shall we?" she said, sliding onto the warm upholstery of the seat.

"I guess so. I hate to leave her here. She's so alone. Thank you for giving her your notebook and pen. At least she can write now." Amy reluctantly pulled her door closed.

"It was nice of the matron to let her keep them. She didn't have to." Lucia switched on the ignition and gingerly put her hands on the hot steering wheel. "Where to next?"

"I guess we might as well go over to Heritage House. There doesn't seem to be much we can do here until tomorrow."

The exterior of Heritage House resembled an antebellum plantation manor expanded far beyond the normal grandiosity. Lucia counted eighteen white marble pillars holding up the roof of the portico. No wheelchair ramp was apparent. Four magnolia trees were surrounded by a neatly trimmed, lush lawn. All of the visible windows were tightly closed against the heat.

Along the edge of the portico were square white planters filled with roses. The far sides had deep crimson flowers, then the shades lightened as they were closer to the massive entry doors. The roses near the entrance were pure white. There wasn't a faded bloom on any plant.

"Just park anywhere. We'll need to get her key from the front desk, then go around and park in the back in the visitors' spaces. They don't like cars cluttering up the view of the entrance. Ruins the ambiance." Amy hopped out, relieved to be so close to a resting spot. She felt giddy with fatigue and stress. Lucia followed, glancing curiously at the ornate furnishing of the foyer. The eighteenth-century French motif seemed ill-suited to the enormous size of the room. It was completely vacant, which was understandable since the chairs seemed designed more for viewing than for comfort.

Amy pushed open the swinging French doors on the other side of the foyer. Inside was an ample hallway and a small reception desk. A plump, cheerful woman was in deep conversation with a rather unattractive man in his mid-thirties. "I'm Amy Traeger, Meg Traeger's niece. Could I have the key to her apartment, please?"

"Sure, honey. It's terrible, the things going on here," the woman murmured.

"Now just a minute, Mabel," the beefy-faced man interrupted. "The contract is suspended on the Traeger apartment. Nobody goes in there except to clean her stuff out. You can't murder someone and then come waltzing in here like nothing happened. You come back with a moving van and I'll escort you in myself."

"Yes, Mr. Fletcher." The comfortable-looking woman shrugged her shoulders under the cheerful sailboats on her cotton blouse. "I'm real sorry, Miz Traeger. Good luck to you and your aunt."

"Wait a minute," Amy said firmly. "I want to talk to Sam Pettigrew. He's the director. He'll let us in."

"He's gone for the day," Fletcher said with a note of gloating in his voice. "I'm the boss when he's gone. Now get out of here. This is private property. I'll have you arrested if you don't leave. The sheriff is a friend of mine."

Amy stood there for a moment, then gathered her tattered rage together for an explosion. Lucia grabbed her arm and tugged. "Come on, Amy. We'll deal with this tomorrow when you're rested." She led the stunned woman outside to their rental car.

TUESDAY

Andrew Byrd ignored the clatter of breakfast dishes that echoed in the twelve-story emptiness above the Atrium Cafe of the Hyatt Mobile. "The sheriff didn't like the idea of a homicide investigator working for the defense, but the DA bought it so there isn't much he could do. I've told them that you'll be by sometime this morning to begin the discovery process. One of my juniors will fax them the forms." He paused in his monologue and looked at Amy. "Do I need to explain the process or should I go on?" He popped a bite of ripe cantaloupe in his mouth while he listened to Amy's reply.

"If the legal process confuses me, I'll straighten it out with Lucia later."

He nodded, taking a sip of espresso. "I also spoke to Sam Pettigrew, the director of Heritage House, this morning. There should be no problem about your staying there if you still want to."

"Impressive," Lucia commented while slicing another bite of sausage.

"I simply reminded him of some of the provisions of the landlord-tenant statutes. Mr. Pettigrew seemed a reasonable person with some experience in legal matters. He was easily persuaded. Of course, I was quite insistent. You can pick up a key from him. I'm anxious to have an investigator on scene because, quite frankly, we need other suspects. The DA briefed me on the evidence, and it's not helpful. Your aunt's fingerprints are all over the kitchen but not on the sugar shaker, which had no prints at all except the victim's. The neighbors report an argument between Ms. Traeger and Mrs. Millett the evening before the homicide. And, worst of all, an empty bottle of digitalis was found in a wastebasket in your aunt's apartment. It was her prescription and the bottle had an unusual amount of powdered digitalis in it. Not good. Not good at all. I'm scheduled to meet with her at 2:30 this afternoon. But, ladies, her best interests will be served with you finding other viable suspects. I've arranged for you to interview her family this afternoon. Remember, all we need is a reasonable doubt. Any questions?" His tone conveyed his expectation that there would be none. There weren't.

"The family members are Lee Millett, his wife Joan, and their son Benjamin. Here is their number at their hotel." He handed Amy a folded slip of paper. "Call me when you have something to report. Good day, ladies." He lay the linen napkin next to the coffee cup and left.

"Is it as bad as I think it is, Lucia?" Amy asked.

"'Fraid so. Motive, means, and opportunity. Meg had them all. It's a strong circumstantial case." Lucia took a forkful of grits and gravy.

"But you can't convict people on circumstantial evidence, can you?" Amy poked idly at the remains of her omelet. The overcooked edges looked even less appetizing than they had a few moments before.

Lucia swallowed, took a sip of orange juice, then answered. "Happens all the time. Most convictions, I would say, depend heavily on circumstantial evidence. No, Byrd is right. We really need other suspects. That's the big weakness of circumstantial evidence. It can fit a lot of people. The digitalis is bad. Very bad. That's a direct link. But it was found in Meg's apartment, not in the murder victim's. That's good. It could be perfectly innocent. Or it could have been planted by someone trying to frame Meg." Lucia ate the last bite of sausage while Amy fished in her wallet for a credit card.

"I think we should call Ruby Sewell. She's obviously a friend of Aunt Meg's. She would probably know a lot about Lorretta. We need a list of other people who would want to have her dead. Especially if they had access to her apartment. Aunt Meg can't be the only person she's had an argument with," Amy said as she handed her credit card to the waiter.

"The digitalis isn't as damaging evidence as a less common drug. There must be dozens of people at that place who use digitalis," Lucia reassured her.

"But why would Aunt Meg have a prescription for digitalis?"

"Doesn't she have a heart problem?"

"Not that I know of," Amy said.

"Then I guess we'd better ask her about that. What do you think Lorretta meant by all that talk about percentages? That really has me mystified."

Amy signed the credit card receipt and pushed back her chair.

"Maybe there will be something in the sheriff's evidence that will help. Shall we go find out?"

Sheriff Beauford Cook did not seem to be in a cooperative mood. His tanned, acne-pocked face was suffused with blood past his hairline. He managed to articulate amazingly well with his jaw rigidly clamped.

"I don't have to give you a damn thing." He pounded his large fist into a pile of papers on the desk.

"If I have to come back here accompanied by the DA it's going to be embarrassing for you, Sheriff Cook. You know that you have to release evidence in a trial. My aunt's lawyer faxed you the proper forms. What is the point in this little display of temper?"

Lucia tried to fade into the Formica paneling on the wall behind her. This approach would not impress her superior as an effort to stay out of another department's hair. Fortunately, all the attention was focused on Amy and no one had noticed that Lucia was in the room.

The sheriff vented some of his rage by hissing through his clenched teeth. "Goddam big-city lawyer. Can't be bothered to drive forty-five whole minutes up to Citronelle to bring the papers himself, now, can he? Law doesn't say I have to take a fax." He hitched up his beige trousers, which had begun to sag over his almost nonexistent hips.

Lucia decided to fling caution to the winds before her lover and the sheriff ended up exchanging punches. "Sheriff Cook, you are absolutely right. There is no requirement for you to accept a fax of the forms. But consider this for a moment. What if Ms. Traeger is found to be innocent? Her niece is running this errand to save her aunt hundreds of dollars that it would cost to pay Mr. Byrd to run the papers over and pick up your file himself. Now, if she is found innocent and word gets out that your actions, which could be construed as harassment, cost her a lot of unnecessary money to prove her innocence...well, some newspapers could have a heyday with that information. I certainly wouldn't want to be vulnerable to the charge that I harassed a little old lady if I was running for reelection. It might not sit well with the retirement community, which I understand is fairly large here in Tensaw County. Some misguided people could even come to think that you were prejudiced against the elderly."

He was visibly deflated. "Ethel Mae, get that file off my desk on the Millett murder. Copy everything and give these girls the copies. Then maybe they'll get the hell out of my business. I'll be up talking to Judge Richards about the

Chestang case if anybody needs me." He stomped out of the office and down the hall.

"He'll be back in a minute or two for his hat. His forehead is real sensitive where his hair don't grow. Best we be done by then," the wispy blond woman almost whispered. She ran with rapid, jerky steps into his office and returned with a manila file folder. The ancient copier set up a racket as it worked, but the slick, warm copies were legible. "That's sixty-seven dollars, please?" She made the request into a question.

"What?" Amy said, outraged.

"Just pay her, Amy," Lucia urged. "I'll explain later."

"Cash?" the receptionist asked.

"What?" Amy yelled.

"How about traveler's checks?" Lucia countered, crossing her fingers.

"Sure," the woman said with obvious relief.

Lucia nudged Amy gently with her elbow. Very stiffly Amy withdrew the pack of traveler's checks from her briefcase and filled out a fifty and a twenty. Wordlessly, the blondc gave her the still-warm stack of papers, then she filled out a receipt and gave change.

"Thank you very much," Lucia said, piloting Amy out the door.

They took the elevator up to the jail. "Try not to aggravate these people, Amy. They're just doing their jobs the best way they know how."

"It's ridiculous and unfair. He's an excrement on the face of law enforcement," Amy replied bitterly.

The elevator door slid open. Amy strode out. Lucia followed more slowly. The matron was a different one from the night before. She was younger, smaller, and paler. She did not seem as gifted with an open, trusting nature as Matron Sullivan.

"Can I help you folks?" she asked. "It's not visiting hours yet," she said, gesturing to the posted sign.

"We're with Andrew Byrd's office. He's representing Ms. Margaret Traeger. He's asked us to get the answers to a few brief questions before his appointment," Lucia said in her most official voice. "Is that a problem for you?"

"No, I guess not. You need to be gone by 11:15, though. That's when we start serving lunch. Nobody from the outside on the unit during meals, right?"

"Certainly," Lucia agreed instantly, blocking Amy's almost-voiced objection. "We'll just leave our briefcases here on the desk." She opened hers and took out the new notebook and pen and the small bag of toiletries they had purchased at Target on their way out of Mobile. "We brought Ms. Traeger a few things like a brush and shampoo, some hairpins, a sweater. If it's within the rules we'd appreciate you checking them, then giving them to her. I know she'd like to look her best when meeting Mr. Byrd." She placed the grey and red plastic bag on the desk.

The matron nodded. "No hairpins," she said, and gestured for them to follow her down the grey linoleum floor of the hall. As they fell behind her, Lucia leaned over and whispered to Amy, "Be cool, professional." Amy nodded, wiping a small tear out of her left eye.

Meg was much calmer than the day before. She had managed to sweep her long silver-brown hair into a crude knot and had tucked most of the wisps of hair into it. Her eyes were no longer puffy. She looked rested, although still very tense. The previous day's distraughtness had disappeared.

"Oh, I'm so glad to see you. I've filled that notebook you brought with everything I could think of about Lorretta," she began, then fell silent at the shake of Lucia's head. All three waited quietly until they were sure the matron was out of earshot. "Here, sit next to me, dear," Meg said, pulling Amy onto the bunk.

"We brought you a sweater. Not one of yours. We couldn't get into your apartment last night. I hope it fits."

Amy put her arm around Meg's waist and hugged her hard.

"It will be fine, Amy. The lawyer is coming by at two to talk to me, the matron says. You didn't happen to bring a new notebook, did you?"

Lucia looked at the one in her hands and nodded. She had tried to settle into a comfortable position on the cold, hard floor. "Wonderful," Meg continued. "It was quite a help, having something to do other than stare at a wall. I do wish I had a window. It's so disorienting, not having any idea what time it is. The matron says I'm not allowed a watch or anything personal for forty-eight hours. I suppose they're checking my belongings for drugs or a hacksaw."

"Suicide prevention. Studies show that prisoners are less likely to attempt suicide if they are stripped of all belongings for the first few days. It also creates a better 'climate of compliance,'" Lucia explained.

Meg laughed nervously. "Well, I certainly want to be compliant. Jail is a very frightening place. Much of last night a woman was screaming. I've no idea why, but it did make sleeping difficult."

"Meg, do you have a prescription for digitalis?" Lucia asked.

"Yes, I do." Her voice fell to a whisper. Terror crossed her face as she withdrew from Amy's embrace.

"Why didn't you tell me you had a heart problem?" Amy asked. "Is it serious?"

"It's minor, and I didn't want to worry you. It's such a boring thing when old people go on and on about their health. It didn't seem important. But I suppose it is important now, isn't it?" She looked fearfully at Lucia.

"It's not good. It means you had access to the murder weapon. Are there other things you didn't want us to know about because it might worry us? It's important to be frank with us, Meg." Lucia rested her head on the white paint that covered the concrete wall and looked up directly into Meg's tearing brown eyes.

"I had to get a refill early on my prescription last Wednesday because I couldn't find my bottle of pills. I suppose I just left them somewhere, but I don't carry them around, you know. I usually leave them in the bathroom to take when I brush my teeth. I have to brush several times a day with one of those electric brushes or I get gum disease. I don't know where I could have put them, but I'm getting used to the fact that my memory isn't great anymore." Several large tears welled over onto her broad cheekbones and slid down her face. "It's all so terrible."

"Aunt Meg, could someone have gotten into your room and taken your pills?" Amy asked putting her arm back around Meg's waist.

"I suppose." She sounded doubtful.

"Does anyone else have a key to your apartment?" Lucia asked.

"Oh, yes. We all give each other keys. Everyone loses them and they make a dreadful fuss at the desk when you ask for a new key. Ruby has one, of course. And Minerva and Helen. Then the maid has to have one to get in. And the front desk, of course. Even Lorretta and I exchanged keys. She's perfectly honest, if not terribly pleasant." Meg had become more animated during her explanation. Then the enormity of what she'd said dawned on her. "Oh dear, that doesn't look good, does it? That I have a key to her apartment."

"No, I wouldn't volunteer that bit of information," Lucia said dryly as she noted it in her notebook. "In fact, it's a very good idea not to say anything at all. Just let your lawyer talk."

"I don't think I'll tell him anything." Meg sounded worried.

"You can tell him whatever you want. He's like a priest; he can't tell anyone," Lucia answered.

"I know, dear. I was a lawyer. But I went to a priest once, when I was in college. I thought it might help my terrible guilt. He told the Dean of Women what I had told him. I suppose he thought it would be helpful, but it was absolutely devastating. Just horrible."

Amy looked at her aunt's profile. "How terrible. I had wondered why you never sought professional help. You could't trust anyone, could you?" Meg shook her head.

"But you weren't Catholic, were you?" asked Lucia.

"No. I suppose that was the loophole, but it just never occurred to me to worry about such things. I was very naive."

The door to the cell opened. "Lunchtime. You girls clear out," the matron said brusquely.

Lucia tore the pages she had used out of the steno pad and handed it to Meg in exchange for Meg's full notebook. "We'll try to be back soon."

Amy hugged her aunt and rose from the cot.

On their way down, Amy asked, "It's getting worse, not better, isn't it?" Lucia nodded in silent agreement. Nor did she speak until they got to the rental car. Once they were inside with the windows rolled up and the air-conditioning on, Lucia dropped her official posture. She put both hands on the top of the steering wheel.

"I know you're scared for your aunt, Amy. It makes you really reactive. But these folks haven't been out of line, except the sheriff about the fax stuff. They could be making our life much, much more difficult. If we make them angry, it only makes things hard for us and for Meg." She craned her neck around to check before she backed out of the parking space. Seeing it was clear, she put her foot on the gas a little heavier than was sensible. The car shot backwards.

"They have all the power, is what you're saying."

"Yeah. That's the bottom line." She pulled back onto Route 45.

"So it's okay to cheat us on the price of copies."

"No, that's not okay. But it is standard practice. I don't know why everybody associated with the law has decided to charge a hundred or two hundred times the going price for copies, but they all do. Wait till you get a bill from your lawyer. Copies will be fifty cents or a dollar there too. It's just one of those stupid aggravations of daily life." Lucia turned right onto the highway to Mt. Vernon.

"So you're telling me to let go of it."

"It would help if you could. It would make things easier for me. But if you can't, you can't. I'll just have to live with it. I need to stop at that ice house for a new notepad. You need anything?" she asked, pulling into the lot of a convenience store.

"No, but I don't think these places are called ice houses anywhere except San Antonio," Amy commented.

"True. When in Alabama, do as the Alabamians do." She disappeared through the double glass doors. By the time she returned, Amy was in the middle of the yellow pages at a pay phone.

"I found a place that sends faxes. It's back on 45. I'll feel better when we get this police report to Byrd," she said.

"Good idea. Then we don't have to chase down to Mobile again," Lucia replied, clutching a handful of notebooks.

Sam Pettigrew extended a firm handshake. There seemed to be genuine welcome in his voice as he said, "Miss Traeger, I'm so very sorry for the rudeness you encountered here last evening. I've already spoken to Rex Fletcher about it and he asked me to give you this note of apology." He extended a business envelope with Amy's name on it.

"We are all under stress, of course," he continued. "But that is never an excuse for rudeness."

Amy smiled up at his wide blue eyes. The wire-rim glasses and old-fashioned haircut gave a slight aura of monkishness to his six-foot frame.

"Thank you, Mr. Pettigrew. This is my associate, Lucia

Ramos. She will be helping my aunt's defense attorney with an investigation."

Lucia nodded at him. "Is there any problem with my talking to people here?"

"I checked with our attorney and he feels it would be best to talk with him rather than our staff." He smiled at her. "I'm sure you can understand."

Lucia winced internally but didn't show it. Not being able to flash a badge was going to make the investigation more difficult. "Certainly," she responded, with no real intention of acceding to his request. His lawyer was less than useless to her investigation.

"Could we have the key?" Amy asked.

"Of course." He took the key from the corner of his mahogany desk. "I just need you to sign this waiver."

Amy read through the paper and returned it to him. "I regret that I can't sign this. It would prohibit me from talking to any residents. Since that is exactly what I plan to do and what is my legal right to do, that is what I will do."

A small frown creased Mr. Pettigrew's forehead. "We are only trying to avoid discomfort for our residents. We can't very well welcome someone inside only to have them hound the people who have paid us to protect them from discomfort."

"Murder is very uncomfortable for all concerned, Mr. Pettigrew. And you were not successful in protecting Mrs. Millett or Ms. Traeger while they were residents. It would be very unpleasant if we have to resort to a court order to enforce Ms. Traeger's contract. It would be likely to focus even more negative publicity on Heritage House." Lucia paused.

"We wouldn't want that. There has been quite enough unpleasantness already." He held the heavy key toward Amy. "Do you know the way to your aunt's apartment?"

"Yes, I visited her here several months ago," Amy replied.

"I hope your stay is pleasant. Now, if you'll forgive me, I have work to do." He ushered them out the door.

Lucia dropped her green soft-sided bag next to the love seat in Meg's apartment. She looked at the two-cushion length and sighed. "Think I'll sleep on the floor," she said.

"You will not, Lucia. You'll sleep in a regular bed like a regular person," Amy said, gesturing toward the bedroom. "Put your bag in there where it belongs."

"Amy, I promised you a year ago I'd never pressure you about being in your bedroom with you. You need to feel safe. I know that what your father did made it hard for you to feel safe in your bedroom unless you were alone and the door was locked. It's okay. I don't mind...too much."

"My sweet Lucita, I want to try this. I had been planning on experimenting with you in my bedroom. I guess this little apartment is as good a place as any to give it a try. You're not my father. I know I can trust you. I didn't know that a year ago." Amy took Lucia's hand and pulled her into the bedroom. "See, twin beds. I remembered that from the last time I was here." Amy stroked the maroon silk comforters. "These were in Aunt Meg's guest room in Chicago. I would stay with her when my parents went to conferences. It was heaven."

"If you're sure it's okay..." Lucia said, putting her bag next to the bed.

"It couldn't be a better place to try you sleeping in my bedroom. It's a thousand miles away from Evanston and it reminds me of the only place I slept that was safe." Amy sat on the edge of the far bed, stroking it lightly with her fingertips. "Meg lived in this ancient but elegant apartment house near the north end of Lake Shore Drive. The building wasn't centrally air-conditioned, so every room had an air conditioner. If it was the least bit hot, I would turn the air conditioner on full blast so I could sleep under this comforter.

"Did you sleep in the same room as your aunt?"

"No. I hated the thought of anyone else in the room while I was sleeping." Amy sat on the edge of the bed and kicked her shoes off.

"I guess after everything your father did, that makes sense."

"Oh, it wasn't just my father. I hated to sleep in the same room as my mother too."

"I would have thought that would have made you feel safe, to have your mother in the same room," Lucia commented in surprise.

"Well, for one thing, she snored, which reminded me of my father. I could never fall asleep until after she did. I was afraid I would say or do something in my sleep. It's so uncontrollable, what you do in your sleep. She hated me being uncontrolled. I could always be controlled during the day, but in my sleep...in my dreams. I was afraid she might be able to read my dreams like she seemed to read my mind when I was a child. 'Put that cookie back.' How did she know?" Amy put her overnight case on the floor near the sink.

"I know now that she knew my habits, my weaknesses. Or maybe I made a noise while trying to sneak around. So why am I still afraid? I don't know." Lucia watched Amy and tried to nod in the appropriate places. She wasn't sure any comment would be helpful.

"In your sleep you are defenseless," Amy continued. "And I needed defenses against the mother who ran her thumbnail down my spine and switched my tiny legs for punishment. I'm an adult now, but in my sleep I'm often a child. But I can trust that child with you, Lucia." Amy seemed to have run through the energy of her emotions. She lay down on the bed.

"Absolutely, querida. Why don't you rest while I put

some notes on the case together?" Lucia came over to her and kissed her sweetly on the forehead. "A little nap would be a good idea. You've been under a lot of stress."

Ten minutes of light sleep seemed to do Amy a world of good. When she wandered back into the living room her eyes sparkled. She rumpled Lucia's hair as she got to the dining table, then she peered over Lucia's shoulder at the papers spread out in front of her.

"Any great discoveries?" she asked, still running her fingers through Lucia's black locks.

"Nope. Pretty much what the lawyer told us," Lucia said.

"I think I should call Ruby Sewell. We need to talk to someone who knows what's going on at Heritage House. I have the feeling that detestable twerp who threw us out of here last night..."

"Rex Fletcher," Lucia offered.

"Yes, Rex Fletcher is going to try to keep people from talking to us," Amy said in a huff.

"Well, as sales manager, it's his job to make Heritage House as attractive as possible. I don't think he views a murder investigation as attractive," Lucia commented.

"Stop being reasonable, Ramos, and get back to work." Amy kissed Lucia on the ear.

"When you set a time to talk to Ms. Sewell, why don't you make it later in the afternoon so we can talk to the Millett family first. They're really my top priority."

"I know," Amy replied. "Most murders are committed by family members." She opened the front pocket of Lucia's briefcase and withdrew the notes they had made in San Antonio. Ruby's phone was answered immediately. The sweet tenor voice seemed very pleased to get the call. Amy explained that Meg was doing as well as could be expected and asked if they could drop by to discuss the case later in the day. Ruby agreed to a 4:30 appointment. "Done," Amy said with satisfaction.

Lucia turned her attention back to the copies of the police report and Amy wandered over to the tan recliner across from the TV set.

"I wonder how they have room for two tables of bridge in here. There's so much furniture for a small room." She pushed her chair into a reclining position and picked up the black enamel kaleidoscope off the end table next to her lounger. "I've never seen one like this." She examined the carved lucite tube projecting like a crescent moon from one end. It was filled with multicolored beads of assorted sizes and shapes. "Oh," she sighed, looking through the viewer, "it's lovely. The shapes change very slowly, like a mandala. This is the most relaxing kaleidoscope I ever saw. I feel like I should be saying a mantra while I watch. Oh, here is a lovely pattern, a red and fuchsia center with green petals, then iridescent red, metallic blue streaks up to soft lavender. I wish you could see it. Maybe if I'm very careful." Amy twisted her whole body so the kaleidoscope moved very slowly.

Lucia knelt next to her and peered through the viewer. "I don't know if it's what you saw, but it's definitely great," she said, releasing the black tube.

Amy slowly turned the kaleidoscope back to her own eye. "Yes, it is the same. I love this. How wonderful, being able to share the patterns." She turned it slightly. "Yuck. Here's one in yellow and olive green." She offered the tube to Lucia.

"If you think I'm kneeling here to look at ugly, you're wrong." She shook the tube like a ketchup bottle before looking. "All black." Lucia tipped it up slightly. "Hmm, looks like three lovely uteruses...uteri?"

"I don't believe you," Amy giggled.

"Yep. See for yourself." Lucia handed the tube back to Amy very gently.

"My goodness, it certainly does. That does rather lead my mind in a certain direction." She ran her fingers underneath and up through Lucia's hair. "Could I talk you into some afternoon delight?"

"Absolutely, querida. But I don't think we should interrupt your lovely patterns. Why don't you just keep looking?" Lucia slid her fingers under Amy's blouse.

"Yes, very nice," Amy said.

"My touching or the kaleidoscope?" Lucia said, cupping Amy's breasts and running her thumbs over Amy's nipples.

"Both," Amy said, arching her back. "It's a very complex pattern of mostly red with...well, almost like mouths opening and closing. Oh, yes," she said, as Lucia caught her nipple between thumb and forefinger. "Definitely yes. Perhaps even a bit harder." She pressed her thighs tightly together and squeezed rhythmically. "Now it's orange circles with hundreds of tiny pink tongues around the edge."

"Lovely notion," Lucia said, lifting Amy's blouse above her breasts, "except I only have one tongue." She licked Amy's swollen nipples until they glistened like the beads in oil inside the lucite.

"One is quite sufficient," Amy said, in a lower pitch. "Quite." She gasped as Lucia caught a nipple between her tongue and teeth. "It's light spring green with little lips everywhere opening and closing. Oh, yes, very nice," she said, crossing her ankles.

Lucia blew on her moist, erect nipples. They tightened.

"Bite me," Amy pleaded. "I want your teeth on me." Lucia complied, taking the cool nipple into her warm mouth and biting it gently.

Amy turned the kaleidoscope rhythmically. "Purple and red and breastlike pink with blue nipples, and yes, I want you inside me."

Lucia slid her hand between Amy's pants and the soft

curve of her belly. She toyed with the edge of Amy's hairs as Amy opened her thighs and pressed up toward Lucia's strong fingertips.

"You are a tease, Lucia Ramos," Amy complained.

"Hmmm," Lucia agreed without moving her teeth from Amy's breast.

"Oh, this looks like the inside of a tunnel. A pink and turquoise tunnel." Lucia let her fingertip graze Amy's swollen clit. "Lower, much lower," Amy said, dropping the kaleidoscope.

She pulled the recliner into an upright position as Lucia shifted to directly in front of Amy's open thighs. She slid her arms under Amy's knees until she could grasp Amy's buttocks and draw her to the edge of the chair. Amy slid one leg out of her underpants. She rested her legs on Lucia's strong shoulders.

Lucia bent her head into the warm fragrance of Amy's desire. Her tongue flicked back and forth, in and out, seeking the rhythm of Amy's rapid deep breaths.

"Yes, querida. Oh, yes," Amy murmured. With both hands she pulled Lucia's head even closer. Lucia began to pant as she slid her fingers deep inside Amy. She moaned with the pleasure of Amy's lust.

Amy crashed into orgasm, drawing Lucia on top of her as the lounger flopped back into a recline position. She drew a few shuddering breaths, then swiftly unbuttoned Lucia's shirt. "I want to taste your breasts," she said, drawing both nipples into her mouth at once. She thrust her knee between Lucia's legs, feeling the quickening rhythm.

Lucia's arms trembled, then she too collapsed in an orgasm, moaning a deep, shuddering cry. Amy caressed her back and head as she rested. "It is always such sweet sex with you, Lucia. So very sweet."

Lucia, with some difficulty, shook off the thought of a quick nap being cuddled on Amy's soft body. She snuggled a moment longer, then got up. She kissed the tip of Amy's nose. "You called me 'querida'. You've never done that before. I like it." She caressed Amy's face with her fingertips scented with the rich muskiness of sex. "And yes, it is sweet sex, sweet as azucar, mi corazón." Lucia smiled and sighed, then returned to her work on the dining table.

"I guess I'd better take a shower," Amy said, laughing as she struggled out of the recliner.

"Good idea," Lucia agreed, breathing deeply of the scent on her hand. "Then maybe we should think about lunch."

"But you've already eaten," Amy protested, kissing her earlobe as she passed.

"High-protein snacks fill the soul but not the stomach," Lucia shouted over the sounds of the shower. She did not expect a response.

She sorted out all the pages that pertained to the autopsy. The final toxicology report wasn't in yet, but the preliminary one, completed on Sunday, was very clear in identifying the presence of digitalis. "Death consistent with the known effects of an overdose of digitalis." She wondered how much it was going to cost Tensaw County for a toxicology done outside of regular office hours. "Plenty," she guessed.

Lucia rummaged through her papers until she found Meg's telephone directory. Dr. Fuller's extension was listed under "Medical Center." A man's voice answered the phone. "Dr. Fuller, this is Lucia Ramos. I'm investigating the circumstances around Lorretta Millett's death. I have a few questions...."

"Are you with the police?" he asked suspiciously.

"No, not here in Alabama," Lucia admitted.

"Talk to Sam Pettigrew. He's the director." The line went dead.

Lucia shrugged and hung up. Then she went through the initial police interviews. Quite a few people seemed to know that Meg and Lorretta Millett argued the night before the murder but only one couple, the Hoskins, who lived across the hall, seemed to have heard it. Lucia wondered at the rapidity of the gossip in Heritage House.

All the remaining members of the bridge club who were in town had been interviewed by the police. The general tone—including Meg's—was "How terrible. I can't imagine who!" Only Dorothy Hoffman's statement was different. She had given a lengthy list of people who had reason to dislike Lorretta. She had even included herself on the list. No employees had been interviewed. No Heritage House staff had been interviewed, except Rex Fletcher. The sales manager, who seemed to live on premises, gave a whiney statement very concerned about protecting the image of Heritage House.

She didn't notice that Amy had gone past her into the kitchen until she was startled by Amy's voice.

"Ruby must have cleaned out the perishables," Amy said, walking out of the small kitchen. "I can't imagine Aunt Meg without lettuce. There's cabbage, though. We could have some soup and coleslaw for lunch."

"Sounds fine." Lucia watched Amy take two steps back to the small white refrigerator and open it. "So, how do we find out about Lorretta Millett? Nobody cares if I am a cop. They don't have to talk to me." Lucia sat at the mahogany table, opening her notebook.

"Who would you talk to if they did care, I mean if you were on the police force here?" said Amy, vigorously attacking a purple cabbage with a butcher knife.

"Her family, her neighbors, her maid, her doctor, her hairdresser. Everyone."

"Well, let's do it. There's a directory in the drawer under the phone in Aunt Meg's bedside table. The worst that can happen is they say no."

Lucia returned with the eight-page directory. "Mrs. Millett lived in A141. There's a map of the grounds in here. It seems to be right down the hall from here." She began to take notes.

"Distressingly convenient," Amy said. She put a couple of heaping tablespoons of mayonnaise in a flowered cup. Then she poured in some of the juice from a bottle of sweet pickles and stirred. She rummaged the spice shelf until she found a bottle of caraway seeds. Rubbing a generous pinch of them between her palms to release the flavor, she dropped them in the cup of dressing. "Those front apartments like Lorretta's are only slightly larger than this one and have the same floor plan."

"I think I remember a sketch in the sheriff's report." Lucia flipped through the papers in her extra-wide briefcase. "Yes, here it is. It does look like the same floor plan, only flipped over so the kitchen is on the right, not the left, of the entry door. It looks like the victim was probably sitting about where I am when she was murdered."

"Do you want to move?"

"No, but don't serve any cinnamon toast with lunch, please." Lucia skimmed the rest of the report.

Amy appeared at the door with a half-opened can of Cross and Blackwell's cream of white asparagus soup in her hand. "Is this okay?"

"Sure," Lucia said. "Well, I don't see much in the crime scene that will help. The fingerprint list is mostly blank. It will probably take a couple more days for it to come back from the FBI. So far, the only matches listed are Lorretta Millett and Margaret Traeger."

"Damn, damn, and double damn," Amy muttered as she stomped back into the tiny kitchen.

"We'll get her off, Amy." Lucia tried to reassure her. "This isn't an ironclad case. There are no witnesses. No direct link of evidence. If she weren't gay..." Lucia let her voice trail off. She flinched with the sound of a pot clashing on a burner.

"That hemorrhoidal pimple of a sheriff has a permanently protruding male appendage stuck where his freeze-dried brains should be." There was another, quieter crash, sounding like an empty can hitting a metal trash receptacle.

Lucia tried to hide her smile. Amy's sense of humor didn't always coincide with her own, and this seemed a bad time for a clash. "Here's a list of books they found on the table near Lorretta's body. It sounds really bizarre to me. What do you think?" Lucia read the list. *"Project Management for Investment Banking, Gracious Homes of the Gulf Coast, Peterson's Guide to Southeastern Song Birds, Mobile Telephone Directory.* I wonder if there were any notes in that. Let's ask Byrd if he can take a look at it."

"Good idea," Amy said, walking toward the table with gold-rimmed white plates. "What would you like to drink: tea, coffee, or water?" She set two places on the empty side of the table, so Lucia wouldn't have to move her papers.

"Water. With ice, please. The rest of the books are *Financial Management for Health Care Institutions, Audubon: Odd Prints and Comments,* and *Striving: A Pictorial History of the 1936 Olympics.* This is a very strange list of books, don't you think?" Lucia asked Amy. She looked up from her placement of silverware and napkins.

"Yes, it is. Is that all of them?"

"Nope. There's a Bible, a *Physician's Desk Reference,* a *Merk Manual,* an *Oxford Unabridged Dictionary,* and *Roget's Thesaurus.* I bet those were on her bookshelf. These were all found in her living room. On her bedside table was *Journal of a Solitude."*

"The book Aunt Meg gave her. Doesn't pay to be kind, does it?" Amy asked, going back into the kitchen for the soup and the slaw.

"I guess not. Not if it gets you accused of murder. Which it doesn't very often, you'll have to admit." Lucia moved to the other side of the table. "Need some help?"

"Sure. Get the drinks, please. Then we're ready to eat." Amy passed her, carrying a couple of large white coffee mugs full of soup. Then Amy returned to the kitchen for the slaw. It looked quite festive with the purple and white shreds clearly visible through the glass dish. Amy set it between them.

"You wouldn't think soup would taste good on such a hot day, but it does," Lucia commented

"Actually, it's not hot in here at all. I think they keep it at a constant seventy-two degrees. How do you like the slaw?"

"Great. What are the little seeds? Tastes a little like anise but not so strong."

"Caraway. Now you know all my secrets," Amy teased.

"No, not by a long shot. You are still a constant mystery. I have never known anyone who surprised me as often as you do, querida. You never talk about what you do when I'm not with you. For all I know you could be a stripper." Amy laughed out loud. "Well, you could be. With your beautiful breasts you could make a million dollars, easy."

"Echas flores, Lucita. Me gusta mucho," Amy replied.

"Your Spanish is really improving. Hang around me and you'll soon be ready for the Spanish Institute." Lucia picked up Amy's hand and kissed her fingers, one at a time.

"Keep that up and we won't talk to the Milletts. Which reminds me, where did I put their phone number?"

"In the little pocket for business cards in your briefcase. But finish your lunch. Five or ten more minutes isn't going to matter. Besides, I want to read you the police interview with them before we see them."

Amy nodded, finishing her mug of soup. "You read while I wash the dishes. I don't want Meg to come home to a dirty kitchen." They each crunched the last few bites of coleslaw in silence.

Lucia carried her dishes in to the sink, then returned to the table to read the tiny stack of reports on the family of Lorretta Millett.

"The first one is a transcript of the phone call from Joan Millett. It's dated Saturday. She's described in the report as the victim's daughter; then someone has written in above the typing 'in-law'. It's short and sweet. 'I'd like to report a suspicious death.' 'Who?' 'Mrs. Lorretta Millett.' 'Where?' 'Heritage House in Mt. Vernon.' 'Yeah, I know where that is. When did she die?' 'This morning, I believe.' 'What's suspicious about it? She stabbed or choked or something?' 'No, but I'm her daughter-in-law. I would like to request an autopsy.' 'If that's what you want. I'll call Doc Roberts. He's the medical examiner. Don't mess with the body. Say, you're sure she's dead? Doesn't need an ambulance or anything?' 'Quite sure. And the doctor at the medical center here agrees, although he feels the death was natural.' 'I see. Well, Doc Roberts will be by sometime soon.' That's it." Lucia numbered that page A-1 and opened her notebook.

"Dr. Fuller from here at Heritage House thought it was a natural death, and she called anyway. I wonder why? Most people would accept the word of a doctor." Amy's voice came out of the kitchen.

"Right. And the call was made within an hour of the official time of death, which is listed between 7:50 a.m. and 8:10 a.m. The steady temperature in this building was probably a real help in getting that short a window of time." Lucia jotted a few notes down.

"We need to see if Aunt Meg has an alibi."

"Yep. Ready for her statement?" Lucia said, picking up the next sheet of paper.

"Yes. Go ahead." Amy came to the door, wiping her hands on a tea towel. "I'm going to let the soup pan soak a minute." She sat in the captain's chair across from Lucia.

"This was taken by the officer who came with the ME. 'Mrs. Joan Millett states that she found the body of Mrs. Lorretta Millett at 8:30 a.m. precisely. She had come by to get Mrs. Millett for a drive to Gulf Shores, planned the day before at dinner. When there was no response to her knock, she opened the door with the key Mrs. Millett had given them several years ago upon their first visit to Heritage House.'"

"They had a key," Amy said, slapping her palms against the table. "They had opportunity. They probably inherit. They have motive."

"Might have motive," Lucia gently corrected her. She continued to read. "'The body was found in a supine position close to a chair pushed out from her dining table. Other than to check for pulse, the body was not moved. Mrs. Joan Millett pulled the emergency cord, and Dr. Charles Fuller pronounced Mrs. Lorretta Millett dead at the scene at approximately 8:45.

"'A discussion ensued as to the cause of death. Dr. Fuller felt it was a heart attack. Mrs. Joan Millett maintained that it could not have been. She insisted that the body not be moved and that the police be called to do an autopsy. Mrs. Joan Millett ordered everyone to leave the apartment and locked the door. She was joined, at that point, by her husband and son, whom she let into the apartment to view the body. They were inside for less than two minutes. All returned to stand outside the door. When no police showed up within ten minutes, she ascertained that they had not been called. She entered the apartment and made the call herself.

"'When the medical examiner arrived, she stated that she was unsure of the cause of death but "it sure as hell wasn't a heart attack". The body was removed to Tensaw County Health Facility morgue for investigation. Mrs. Joan Millett, under questioning, stated that she knew of no reason to think foul play was involved nor could she think of anyone with a reason to kill her mother-in-law.

"'Names and addresses of all present were taken and they were asked to stay close until the results of the autopsy were in. Then the next interview was done on Sunday, after the digitalis was discovered in her stomach.

"'Mrs. Joan Millett states that she had no reason to suspect digitalis poisoning. She simply knew that Mrs. Lorretta Millett had not died of a heart attack. She was with her husband and son driving up from Gulf Shores to pick up her mother-in-law at the time of death. She, her husband, and her son were all present in the victim's apartment on Friday at lunchtime. All three had access to the sugar shaker at that time. Mrs. Joan Millett has had no argument with the victim. She states that her husband "hasn't bothered to argue with his mother in twenty years". Her son "badgered his grandmother for a large sum of money to invest, but no one took the request seriously". The large sum of money was said to be $250,000. Mrs. Joan Millett knows of no one with a grudge against her mother-in-law or any reason to kill her.' End of interview." Lucia put down the unpleasantly slick copy she had been reading from. "What do you think?"

"They didn't even need a key. They were in the apartment anyway. I can't imagine Joan Millett had anything to do with the murder. Why would she contest the opinion of the House doctor if she did? Come to think of it, why was she so sure it wasn't a heart attack? It doesn't make sense, so I guess we can't rule her out yet. She may be some sort of psychopath who enjoys flirting with danger. I think the grandson is awfully interested in a lot of money. That's worth remembering. Not much else. How about you?"

"Pretty much what you got. That phrase, 'he hasn't bothered to argue with his mother in twenty years' is a little weird. Let's read his statement next. He talked less. 'Lee Millett also knew of no one with a grudge or a reason to kill his mother. He spontaneously commented that he had not had an argument with his mother in many years because 'her mind was about as open as the doors on a bank vault'. That's it." Lucia looked at the sheet of paper, her puzzlement obvious.

"Awfully short, isn't it?" Amy asked, incredulously.

"Yeah."

"I wonder why."

"I think maybe all the family was interrogated together instead of separately, so he was just adding to what Joan said." Lucia tapped the end of her pen against the report.

"That's not proper procedure, is it?"

"Nope, unless there is little chance of the persons being interviewed being involved in the crime or of having any information to add. For example, if a felon is fleeing though a large crowd, you might take them three or four at a time for questioning since you're not likely to get new information from any one in particular. But in this case, it's pretty bad protocol. The sheriff had obviously decided that the family wasn't involved and knew nothing, a pretty questionable hypothesis."

"I am departing the state of extreme aggravation with that slime and entering into a state of pure hatred." Amy made the statement with no emotion.

"I can see why. Let's move on to the grandson's statement." She picked up the mostly blank sheet of paper. "Then on the other hand, let's not bother. I can summarize it easily. 'I don't know anything.' Great detective work. I'm certainly impressed." She paper-clipped the four pieces of paper together and tossed them in her open briefcase. "Do you want to call the family, or should I?"

"Why don't you?" Amy replied. "I'm too emotional about all this to be at my best. I suppose we'll have to drive to Gulf Shores to see them. How are we going to interview each one alone?"

Lucia rummaged in her briefcase for the phone number. "I don't know. Ask them, I guess. Interesting. This is the same prefix as your aunt's number and Ruby Sewell's. I wonder if they're here today. If they are, why don't we just ask them over here, one at a time?" A smile of relief spread across her brown cheeks. "And let's start with Joan Millett."

The conversation was very brief. She agreed to meet with Lucia and Amy in "a few minutes" and hung up. Next, Amy called Andrew Byrd. He wasn't available, but Ms. Eisenberg said he wanted them to know that the arraignment was scheduled for one o'clock tomorrow afternoon.

She acknowledged that the faxes of the sheriff's file had arrived safely and thanked Amy profusely, assuring her that Mr. Byrd would let her know immediately of any developments.

Roz's voice dropped into an even more soothing tone. "Mr. Byrd wanted you to be aware that the bail is likely to be high, since this is a capital offense. He recommends that you have funds transferred for the ten percent surety bond. You may use our office account to facilitate transfer, and Mr. Byrd will bring the funds with him to court tomorrow. He believes that twenty-five thousand would be safe, as it is unlikely that bail will be set at more than a quarter of a million." She hastened to add, "Of course, it may not be necessary at all. But it's better to be prepared for the worst." She gave Amy the account number.

"They want twenty-five thousand to cover bail," she said to Lucia.

"Wow, a quarter of a million! It probably won't go that high, Amy," she responded. "Better hope we can pay the bond to the court. If we pay it to a bail bondsman, you can kiss it goodbye. That's their fee. They don't give it back like the court does."

"They can do that?" Amy asked incredulously.

"They have to make a living too. A lot of their customers skip out on them. It's not a pleasant career." She was interrupted by a knock at the door.

Joan Millett was a short, lumpy woman with greying red hair. She held her back and shoulders with military rigidity and wore a dark blue linen coat and skirt that seemed almost uniformlike. Amy gestured for her to enter and offered her a chair in the living room.

"I'm Dr. Amy Traeger and this is Detective Lucia Ramos, who is assisting with the investigation." Lucia nodded from her chair at the dining room table.

"Do you mind if we tape this conversation, Mrs. Millett?" she asked.

"No, but I would prefer that you call me Dr. Presley. I never took my husband's name, for professional reasons. 'Mrs. Millett' has always been my mother-in-law and, especially now, it feels uncomfortable to be addressed that way." She settled herself as comfortably as possible into the lounger, unable to fit easily into its generous proportions.

"Would you care for tea, coffee, anything?" Amy asked.

"No. This isn't a social call, and I would like to handle this exchange of information as expeditiously as possible," Dr. Presley declared.

Amy nodded and sat in the rocker next to her. "Frankly, we were a little surprised when you agreed to talk to us. Pleased, but surprised."

"I have agreed to talk to you because you have a very persuasive, if somewhat unpleasant, attorney. He made a very good case for your aunt's innocence. I have to say that the precipitous arrest did seem to preclude a thorough investigation. I find it extremely dubious that Lorretta Winn Millett was murdered as a result of some lesbian love nest. My mother-in-law was not a woman of sexual passion, and it is my impression that people's deaths are usually a logical progression from their lives."

"What would have been the logical death for Mrs. Millett?" Amy gently prodded.

"If she were murdered, it would be for money, not sexual intrigue. Money was the passion of my mother-in-law's life. She was involved with mortgage banking for forty years and money was her main obsession. Please don't misunderstand. She was not a greedy woman and she was the soul of honesty. But money captured most of her attention. It was both her work and her hobby."

"She was a wealthy woman," Lucia commented.

"Quite. It is my understanding that her estate is several million dollars. That does not include the sizable life trust she settled on my husband in the late sixties." Dr. Presley seemed somewhat taken aback at the line of questioning.

Her stubby fingertips with square-cut nails drummed silently against the upholstered arm of her chair.

"With all those years in mortgage banking, I would imagine she made lots of enemies?" Lucia made the statement into a query.

"No, she did not. She considered it a personal reflection on her decision making and management ability if any loans went bad, so she would go to extraordinary personal effort to assist her accounts to maintain current payments. She came to banking under the tutelage of her father-in-law, whose banking practices were so conservative that his bank lost no money during the Depression. He himself amassed a personal fortune by buying up land bankruptcies during that time. That money was the core of Mrs. Millett's estate." Dr. Presley seemed more comfortable with the conversation. She attempted to settle once more into the lounger. "It might have been even larger, but Mrs. Millett always donatedten percent of her income to worthy causes. That, plus taxes, which she never tried to avoid, caused the growth to be slower than it might be under less ethical stewardship."

"She sounds like a very upright person," Amy said.

"Quite so," Dr. Presley agreed.

"Yet she was murdered. I understand you're the one who insisted that an autopsy be done."

"Yes, I was."

"May I ask why?" Lucia asked their visitor.

"For one thing, her face was not contorted with pain. Besides, my mother-in-law had an extremely healthy heart. There was absolutely no reason for her to die of any problem related to her heart." The reply came phrased as absolute, unquestioned fact.

"How could you be so sure?" Lucia questioned.

"She sent me her cardiological workup only two months ago. She was in the habit of having a complete physical annually after she passed the age of sixty-five. She always sent the attending physician's report to me for confirmation."

"Why?"

"Because she always said I was the best cardiologist she knew. It was her opinion that my withdrawal from the active practice of medicine gave me more time to stay abreast of developments in my field. I share that opinion. While I still maintain my license in the state of California, I do not see patients except for the occasional charity patient who presents an interesting case. I do, after all, have a son to raise." She made that statement as if it explained everything.

"But you were a practicing cardiologist?" Lucia probed.

"For six years."

"So you weren't surprised to find your mother-in-law had been poisoned with digitalis?" Amy asked.

"I was totally shocked. I expected the pathologist to find an aneurism or stroke, not poison. Unbelievable! One does not expect a relative to die from the malicious violence of strangers. This isn't a drive-by shooting in East LA. This is murder in a setting which should be one hundred percent free of that type of risk. I helped Lorretta investigate this place, and I feel it is my duty to help clear up her murder." She pounded her small fist into the leather upholstery.

"What did you look into in your investigation of Heritage House?" Amy prodded.

"Ownership, tenant satisfaction, fiscal soundness. That type of information."

"And what did you find out?" Lucia asked as she sat back in her chair.

"Heritage House is owned by a consortium of churches as a wholly owned subsidiary. It is very sound financially. The residents seemed content. Certainly the Alabama tax laws were a major part of her decision to move here. They are very favorable to retirees."

"Do you know who will inherit her estate? Is it your husband?"

"Lorretta was very clear about the inheritance. She always sent us a copy of her will, which she updated regularly when tax laws changed. The entire estate, less some minor bequests, is left in trust to my son Benjamin."

"I see. So neither you nor your husband would profit in any way from Mrs. Millett's death?" Lucia clarified.

"I would receive a small income to compensate me for acting as trustee of my son's trust."

"You would control the estate?" Lucia asked.

"My mother-in-law also had great faith in my fiscal conservatism, a faith which is not misplaced. While my son and husband tend to dream of large financial rewards, I am much more similar to Aesop's ant than the grasshopper."

"Very good. Can you tell me when you last saw Mrs. Millett and what her physical condition appeared to be?"

"We were stopping by for a brief visit on our way home from a business trip to New York. We had lunch with her Friday, and at that time she appeared to be in excellent health. She did seem quite thirsty, having several glasses of water; apparently this wretched heat and humidity takes adjusting to. She seemed in good spirits, if somewhat peeved at the unexpectedness of our visit."

"She didn't know you were coming?" Amy asked.

"My husband is occasionally impulsive. This stop was one of his impulses. Lorretta was able to clear her calendar all of Saturday, but Friday was impossible for her. We found her body at 8:30 on Saturday morning. She was obviously dead. Given the effects of this climate on decomposition, I'm glad it wasn't later. We are having the body cremated, as was her wish. Unfortunately, she left no instructions as to the disposal of the remains. Lee wants to fly them over the Pacific and scatter them, while Benjamin favors leaving her ashes in an urn on the mantel. I consider the one too romantic and the other rather gruesome. I imagine she will simply be interred next to her husband in Oklahoma City. That seems proper."

"Could we go back to something you said earlier?" Lucia asked.

"Certainly."

"You said that you expected a stroke or an aneurysm. Both would be natural causes of death. Why then did you call the police and report a suspicious death?"

"I'm not sure. If I had known another doctor nearby I would have called him, but I don't. In fact, the dearth of county medical facilities other than at Heritage House was one of the slight drawbacks of the facility. It seemed perfectly logical at the time, but in retrospect it does seem an odd choice on my part. I really haven't an explanation other than my being emotionally upset at finding the body of a woman I admired and respected and then having my professional judgment questioned by a nincompoop." Her sentence ended abruptly.

"Nincompoop?" Amy asked.

"That charlatan, Dr. Fuller. When Lorretta moved in, Mrs. Dexter, a delightful and competent physician's assistant, was head of the medical center. She never would have questioned my judgment."

"I see," Amy said.

"Dr. Presley, do you know any of Lorretta Millett's friends here at Heritage House?" Lucia asked.

"No, not really. I know she was in a bridge club because that's why she wasn't free on Friday afternoon. And she mentioned she was having dinner with an Earl Banks. Other than that, no, not at all."

"So you would not be aware of any conflicts she might have been involved with?"

"Naturally not. I'm afraid I've told you all I know. I really must get back to Lorretta's apartment." She rose from her seat and extended her hand to Amy. "I wish you luck in your investigation. Frankly, I don't relish the media version of the theory that my mother-in-law was murdered in a fit of perverted lust. It seems quite improper. Good day."

"Would you ask your son to drop by? We'd like to ask him about his impressions also," Lucia said, standing.

"Certainly." Dr. Joan Presley left the apartment with no hesitation.

"Well, that was certainly informative. Do you think she realized she gave both her husband and her son a motive for murder when she talked about Lorretta's estate?" Lucia asked.

"I doubt it. She doesn't seem to be interested in looking beneath the surface of things and probably doesn't expect others to do so either. A remarkably straightforward person, I would say. Definitely low ranking as a poisoner. But she's given them more than motive, she's provided the method too, if I'm right. I'll bet that she still carries her medical bag with her. And if she does, there's probably..."

"A bottle of digitalis in it. After all, she's a cardiologist!" Lucia exclaimed. "Very good, Detective Traeger. Very good. I'll follow up on that with son Benjamin. What else do you think we should ask him?"

"The money, of course. How he got along with his grandmother. I wonder if Aunt Meg has some frozen lemonade. That's usually a hit with kids." She went into the kitchen to check the tiny freezer compartment of the small refrigerator. "No lemonade. Just frozen okra and frozen carrots. I didn't know Aunt Meg liked okra." Her further comments were interrupted by a knock on the door.

Amy opened the door on a surprisingly tall preadolescent boy wearing a red T-shirt with a pocket, white shorts with matching red trim, and large, red running shoes. His light brown hair was professionally cut and carefully combed.

"I'm Benjamin Millett. Joan said you wanted to speak to me," he announced.

"Thank you for coming over. This is Lucia Ramos and I am Amy Traeger."

"It's okay. We were just clearing out Lorretta's apartment and it's kind of gruesome," he replied.

"I thought it was sealed as a crime scene," Lucia said.

"The sheriff said it was okay. He had everything he needed from it. I've never been in a dead person's apartment before. It's kind of weird." He flung himself on the floor near the dining room table and propped himself against the wall.

"Your grandmother's dead," Amy said softly while pulling a chair out from the table.

"Yeah. Murdered. Too weird. Nobody I know has a murdered grandmother." He started bouncing his back off the wall.

"Does that make you sad?" Amy asked.

"You sound like a shrink. Are you a shrink?"

"Yes, I guess that's why I talk like one." Amy smiled.

"So who do you think killed your grandmother?" Lucia asked.

"I guess that old lady they arrested. The queer. I didn't know there were old queers." Amy winced.

"What if it wasn't her, who would you think might have done it?" Lucia prodded.

"Dad, I guess. He was always fighting with her. He wanted her to invest in the super big project he designed. He's an architect, you know. It's really kind of neat. No highways. Residential core with perimeter shops and offices. Every house is wired into a main frame. Neat. Bad investment, though. Not enough discretionary income in the appropriate target market. It'll go bust. Most of his ideas do. Too much of a dreamer. Good thing his money is in a trust or he would have gone belly up years ago. My portfolio has increased by thirty percent in two years. Not bad for a recession. I could do better if I had a bigger chunk to invest. Fifty thousand dollars is chump change in the market. No leverage at all." He stood up. "I gotta go now. Need to help my parents. Bye."

Amy and Lucia sat openmouthed as he walked out the door.

"Well, that was a great job of controlling the interview, wasn't it?" Lucia remarked. "We didn't even get in the question about the medical bag."

"No, we didn't," Amy replied. "Why do I have the feeling he's been in therapy most of his life? He certainly seemed experienced at answering questions from adults."

"And deflecting them," Lucia said, jotting down a few notes.

"He does seem passionately attached to money."

"Yep. And not a bit surprised at his grandmother's death...oh, and quite willing to turn suspicion toward his father. Not a close family, I would say."

"Most people are killed by relatives. Any of the Milletts had motive and opportunity. But means..." Amy's voice trailed off. "I just wish we had asked him about the bag."

"Joan is a cardiologist. She would have easy access to digitalis whether it is in her bag or not. But if she did it, why on earth would she demand an autopsy? No, I'm inclined to eliminate her on that basis alone. No one would have known it was murder if she had kept quiet. It just doesn't make sense...." Lucia interrupted herself. "We should talk to Lee Millett."

"I'll call him," Amy offered. She checked the number and dialed. "Lee Millett, please. This is Amy Traeger...could we talk about your mother's death? Certainly. We'd be happy to. See you in a moment." She hung up. "Grab your notebook and pen, Lucia. We've been invited to interview Lee Millett in his mother's apartment. Let's go. Maybe we can ask him about his wife's medical bag."

The man who opened the door was short and chubby. If his hair hadn't begun to grey, he would have looked little older than his son. His smile was welcoming, unmarred by a trace of sorrow. Amy expressed her condolences as they shook hands.

"Thank you, but it's rather a relief to have her dead. We never got on well." He gestured them toward a quartet of ladder-back chairs with petite-point seat covers. As they were sitting, Joan Presley came out of the bedroom with a black plastic bag.

"This can all go to Goodwill or the cleaning lady or whatever. You could speak a bit more kindly of your mother, now that she's dead, Lee."

"It's hard to dissimulate even for death, Joan." He turned his guileless eyes back toward Lucia and Amy.

"My mother was a cold woman, interested in nothing except money. I never understood how she had any friends at all. Her first job was foreclosing on mortgages. She loved it."

"Lee, that's not true. She was a librarian when she met your father. Doing research was her passion. I think she viewed delinquent mortgages in the same light as overdue library books that needed to be called in." Joan Presley shook her head as she sat in the fourth chair. Her role as intermediary between mother and son seemed longstanding.

"And she never once considered who she might be hurting, did she?"

"I'm not sure she was capable of seeing that viewpoint. Relationships with people seemed difficult for her," Joan said, reaching over to run her fingers through her husband's disarray of grey curls. As soon as she finished putting them in order, he ran his hand through them again, leaving them disheveled.

"Remember that visit we had from your father's second cousin, Sandra Cummings? She recounted a visit to your grandparents' home when you were a baby. I was quite charmed by her story of your mother swooping you up in her arms, holding you high above her head while she crooned 'baby doll' over and over."

"If it was true," Lee replied bitterly.

"Oh, I'm sure it was, Lee. I recall your mother calling you 'baby doll' on several occasions."

"Oh, she could do just fine when she wanted something from someone. Then she could charm the skin off a snake." He shook his wife's hand out of his hair.

"Your Okie roots are showing." She smiled at Lucia as her husband scowled. "You can take the boy out of Oklahoma, but you can't take Oklahoma out of the boy. But then I've always found Lee's colloquialisms quite delightful. That's why I gave up my career in cardiology to marry him."

"And here I thought it was my burned draft card," he twitted.

"I didn't find that as despicable as your mother did when she disinherited you, but it was hardly attractive. Besides, you'd done that years before we met. I should let these people talk to you uninterrupted while I finish the sorting. Heaven only knows what decisions Benjamin is making in my absence."

"He's probably ranking Lorretta's possessions based on dollar value. If he weren't a boy, I'd wonder if Lorretta had somehow managed to clone herself in my child. Their view toward things is incredibly similar," he commented with mild disgust.

"Do you think your son is capable of plotting his grandmother's death to gain his inheritance?" Lucia asked boldly.

"Probably. He is quite intelligent and quite calculating, but I doubt he would do such a thing."

"Why not?" Lucia asked while jotting notes.

"Against his ethics. Like my mother, he has very rigid ideas of what the rules are and he doesn't break them. That's cheating, and he is not a cheat. I know it seems strange, but both of them were quite consistent in that respect. As is my wife, for that matter."

"And yourself?" Amy interjected.

"I don't play by the rules. I burn draft cards, refuse to be a war hero like my father and older brother. Dead war heroes, I might add. I gamble with other people's money, don't complete PhD's and have a list of profligate vices as long as your arm. Thanks to years of therapy, I now recognize that I am merely human, not evil." He announced this hard-won insight with no small satisfaction.

"You hated your mother," Amy said.

"For many years. But in the last decade, I have allowed myself to understand her more and hate her less. Her rigidity kept her miserably unhappy. I don't believe she had a single joyous moment after my father's death in London during the Blitzkrieg. He wasn't even doing anything heroic, just running down a street, and the wall of a building fell on him.

"My brother, Larry, remembered how happy she was when he came home on leave once. He told me that story over and over again. I never met my father. He died three months before I was born. I suspect, had he lived, my life, our lives, might have been very different." Speaking of his father's death brought the sadness into Lee's face that he could not feel or show over his mother's. Tears began to trickle from the corners of his eyes. "I don't know why I'm crying," he said.

"Perhaps to mourn the family you never had but desperately needed," Amy offered.

"Yes. Excuse me. I really don't want to continue this conversation. Perhaps another time, by phone after we're home." He stood and ushered them to the door.

"This not being able to flash a badge is very frustrating, Amy," Lucia commented as they stood looking at the closed door. "I never got to ask him about the bag."

"Damn, damn, and double damn. Let's just ask him." Amy knocked on the door, which was instantly answered by

Lee. "Mr. Millett, I know this is a real imposition, but I have a devastating headache, and I just wondered if your wife might have something a little stronger than aspirin."

"I'll ask her," he said, somewhat uncertainly. "Joan, do you have something for a headache?" he shouted toward the bedroom.

"I've got some aspirin in my medical bag. It's near the refrigerator on the kitchen counter," came back the reply.

"Thank you, anyway. Aspirin I have lots of." Amy pulled the door closed. Lucia flashed her a huge grin and a thumbs up. She followed the skipping Amy down the hall to a small nook with two chairs in it. Lucia checked her watch.

"We should go on to Ruby Sewell's. It's almost time for our appointment. Do you remember the apartment number or do we need to go back to Meg's for it?" Lucia asked.

"A206, I'm pretty sure. Did you notice the painting above Lorretta's dining room table?"

"No, not really," Lucia replied as they ambled down the plush blue carpeting.

"I think it was a Corot. A small one, but if it is a Corot, it's probably worth more than fifty thousand dollars."

"You're kidding! Surely it would be in a museum or something."

"No, I think she was wealthy enough just to have it there to enjoy. I can't imagine having that much money," Amy commented.

"Says she who drives a Saab. Do you want to take the stairs or the elevator?" Lucia asked as they came to the end of the corridor.

"Stairs. We have the time and it's good for me." Impulsively she took Lucia's hand as they went up the stairs.

"You better be careful or we'll end up accused of murder ourselves. They take queers very seriously here," Lucia joked.

Amy smiled at her and released her hand to open the door at the top of the stairs. A206 was three doors down from the stairwell. Hanging by fishing line from the metal numbers was a thin wooden plaque that said "Ruby Sewell says Howdy." Lucia rapped on the door. It opened immediately.

"Oh, dear, you're not at all what I expected, Amy," said a tiny white-haired woman.

"I'm Lucia Ramos, Ms. Sewell," Lucia said, stepping aside. "This is Amy Traeger."

"Yes, yes. Exactly as Maggie described. I'm so excited to meet you finally." She flung her thin arms around Amy and pulled her down for a peck on the cheek. She then pulled Amy into the apartment. Lucia followed, closing the door behind them. "And just who are you, Lucia Ramos?"

"A friend of Amy's," Lucia answered.

"A very good friend, indeed, to come all the way to Alabama to help her aunt." Ruby patted Lucia's cheek and smiled a knowing smile. "Now you two sit over there on the couch and ask all those questions I'm sure you have." She scurried into the kitchen and returned with a silver bowl full of nuts. "Please, have some glazed pecans. I love to make them, but I can't taste them anymore. So I just enjoy others' enjoyment." She put the bowl on the pine slab coffee table.

Amy and Lucia reached for a nut at the same moment and their fingertips grazed at the bowl. Ruby's smile widened.

"Do you mind if I take notes?" Lucia asked.

"No, I haven't been interviewed in years. I used to do it all the time to others when I was a reporter. Turnabout's fair play." She seated herself in a hand-crafted pine chair below a watercolor of a desert scene.

"The obvious question is, do you know who killed Lorretta Millett?"

"I wish I did. Then Maggie wouldn't be locked up in some hellhole of a jail." Ruby looked quite fierce.

"Do you know who might want to kill her? Who might be

angry at her or jealous, who might profit from her death?" Lucia continued.

"Well, now, that's a whole passel of questions. Let me take them from the top. Just about anybody might want to kill her at one time or another. She was a very aggravating woman, an odd combination of insecurity and arrogance. She assumed everyone had flaws except her. She would just pick at people unmercifully."

"Could you give us an example?" Amy said, before munching another pecan.

"Poor Edith Malone had terrible feet. She's been to dozens of podiatrists and had several surgeries. The most comfortable shoes she can wear are those cheap rubber thongs. The first time she came to the bridge club, Lorretta pointed her feet out to everyone and then commented, 'If my feet were that ugly, I'd want to cover them up so no one would have to look at them.'" Ruby mimicked a very cruel tone of voice.

"Why did anyone have anything to do with her? She sounds vicious," Amy asked.

"She was, sometimes, but she could also be very charming, and we would all forgive her nastiness."

"Perhaps someone wasn't as forgiving. Just how nasty did she get? It seems she threatened Meg with disclosure of some pretty private information," Lucia said.

"Her lesbianism. Yes, she told me. I suppose Lorretta could have done a similar thing to someone less forgiving than Maggie. It's possible," Ruby admitted.

Amy's eyes narrowed. "Wait a minute. You called me from Meg's apartment. If the sheriff let her have a call, why would she have called you unless..."

"She didn't call me, Amy. I was already in her apartment when the sheriff came. I was sleeping over." A wicked grin sped across Ruby's impish face.

"You're more than just good friends," Lucia said.

"We are considerably more than just good friends. We moved here together."

"You're from Chicago?" Amy asked, bewildered.

"No, dear. I'm from Carlsbad, New Mexico." Ruby seemed to be thoroughly enjoying herself.

"New Mexico!" Lucia exclaimed. "How on earth did you meet?"

"Well, the trouble is, I think Maggie is a little ashamed that we met on a cruise. The whole notion of cruising appalls her—at a bar, I mean, not the ship. But I think she feels that I picked her up in a bar. Probably because that's exactly what I did. She was having a scotch and water in the starboard lounge. I sat next to her and asked what a beautiful woman like her was doing in a place like this. I must have been a bit tipsy or I wouldn't have had the courage. She was sitting there, looking almost regal with her glorious silver– brown hair piled up in a bun and that smile of hers. I fell in love the minute I saw her. Just like the movies. You'd never believe what she answered: 'Cruising, of course.' Can you imagine your aunt saying that? Now that I know her, I can't. She was momentarily oblivious to the pun. I still tease her about it. When new friends ask how we met, I always say, 'In a bar, while cruising.' They never believe it of your aunt.

"That night I took her dancing. Linda Collier was singing "Silver-Haired Women" for our first dance. In my mind that will always be our song. Your aunt didn't mind at all that I was shorter. Some women don't like you to lead if you're shorter than they are. But not Maggie. I just snuggled my cheek into those wonderful soft breasts of hers and danced away. You're a lucky woman, Lucia Ramos. I bet that when Amy is Maggie's age, her breasts will be exactly like Maggie's. Not me. I lost what little I was given to breast cancer in my sixties. Always thought I was small-chested until I lost them entirely. I surely wished then that I had never complained. Frankly, I would have rather lost my teeth and kept my breasts, instead of the other way around, but nobody asked my preference."

"Did Lorretta Millett know about your relationship?" Lucia asked.

"I'm not sure. She never spoke to me about it. I don't believe she said anything to Maggie either." Ruby slipped off her shoes and propped her stockinged feet on the coffee table.

"If she didn't know about you, how did she come to accuse Aunt Meg of lesbianism?" Amy asked perplexed.

"Probably because Maggie gave her a book written by a lesbian. It was *Journal of a Solitude* by May Sarton. Maggie's always trying to help people. Mostly it's harmless. But this time..."

"That's what she thought too," Lucia commented. "Do you know any other secrets Lorretta may have held against someone?"

"No, but I did notice some people step pretty careful in her presence. I can't put my finger on it, just seems they have an attitude of not wanting to make Lorretta mad at them." She reached for a pecan. "Sure wish I could still taste these."

"Who?"

"Well, her neighbors, the Hoskinses. Willa Hoskins has never been particularly careful of my feelings, but she walked on eggshells around Lorretta."

"Could you tell us about that last bridge game," Lucia requested. Amy picked up a handful of pecans.

"Well, it was pretty grim, I can tell you that. Lorretta was in a nasty mood. She kept after Dorothy Hoffman like a picador with a bull. Jab, jab, jab. About how Earl was going to have to make up his mind. How she was going to give Earl an ultimatum. Then she started in on your aunt with all these innuendos about the *Journal of a Solitude* or *The Well of Loneliness* and how they looked alike to her and how maybe people need to know whom they are living next to. I just knocked a deck of cards on the floor to distract her. I was really glad to be at the other table. Minerva and I played double sol and thanked our lucky stars we weren't involved. I was happy to leave that apartment."

"Was this typical of the games in her apartment?" Amy asked.

"Nope. I think she was put out by her family showing up. She hated surprises. She was just feeling unusually mean, I guess. Are you girls hungry? I eat early, and I was thinking if you didn't have any plans you all might join me for dinner. I'm just having pasta and pesto with a salad. Come on, humor an old lady and say you'll stay."

Lucia and Amy exchanged glances. Lucia gave a slight shrug.

"We'd be delighted. But only if you'll let us wash the dishes," Amy said.

"You'll have to fight that one out with a machine." When Amy looked perplexed, Ruby continued, "I have a dishwasher, dear."

"Oh. I didn't expect one. Aunt Meg's apartment doesn't have one."

"She didn't feel it was worth the cost of the dishes of one person, once a day," Ruby said, putting her feet squarely on the floor and then pulling herself out of the chair with the arm rests. She stood a little slowly, as if having to consciously move each muscle. "I entertain a lot so I had the dishwasher put in."

"You only eat one meal a day in your rooms?" Lucia asked, also standing.

"Sit. That kitchen is too small for more than one person. Yes, we get two meals a day provided as a part of our rent. Many people eat all three since that would make the third meal breakfast, which is only $3. It used to be $2.50, but they had to raise the price a couple of years ago. I guess the price of prunes must have gone up." Ruby's voice carried from the kitchen into the living room. Lucia and Amy could hear her clearly despite the background sounds of a meal being prepared.

"Do you eat the three meals every day in the dining room or do you switch them around?" Lucia asked hoping Ruby could hear her over the sound of a running faucet.

"Lunch and dinner. If you skip both without letting the front office know, they call your room to be sure you're okay. Just a little double check like the bead program." Ruby stuck her elfin face out of the kitchen to check on her guests' comfort, then ducked back into the dinner preparations.

"Beads?" Lucia asked, mystified. She stopped taking notes long enough to pop another glazed pecan into her mouth.

"They have these short strings of beads like Greek worry beads..." Amy began to explain.

"Or Islamic prayer beads," Ruby interrupted.

"Like a rosary?" Lucia asked.

"Sort of..." Amy hesitated. "A floor monitor checks them each morning and evening. The residents put them out at night and bring them in after breakfast. If they're in the wrong place someone makes sure the resident is okay."

Ruby came out of the kitchen and picked the bracelet-sized string of large multicolored beads off the back of the door. She tossed them to Lucia.

Lucia smiled in appreciation of the accuracy of the throw. "Played a little softball in your day, I'll bet," she commented to Ruby.

"State champions for three years running in the early fifties. I was the pitcher, but the star of the team was this gorgeous redhead named Judy, a young Mormon girl with five kids. She had just come out and she was wild. Her husband had regular shouting matches over her 'wifely duties' at the games. I was so in love with that woman! She ended up starting a nursery business—plants, not babies—and became very successful. We still write and visit. What a ball player! What a woman!" Ruby settled back down in the pine chair. "I hope you don't mind. For salad, I've cut us a wedge of cabbage. I eat a lot of raw cabbage since the breast cancer. It's supposed to help. Of course, it's a bit like locking the barn door after the horses have taken off, but it makes me feel like I'm trying."

"No, it's fine," Amy said, smiling at the knowledge of where the cabbage had come from in her Aunt Meg's refrigerator. "We both like it very much."

"I didn't know it helped with breast cancer," Lucia said.

"Yes, all the cole family help prevent it, like broccoli, cabbage, brussels sprouts. But it's better if you eat them raw." Ruby sighed. "I was such a steak and potatoes person until the cancer. Growing up in ranching country, that's what you ate. Vegetables were foreign fare, except tomatoes and corn in the summer. My poor mother tried so hard to get us to vary our diet, but we'd have none of it, my father and me. Well, if our foresight were as good as our hindsight, life would be boring, now wouldn't it?"

Lucia and Amy nodded their agreement. "I'd like to put some of this information together and please tell me if I've gotten it right," Lucia said. "Let's suppose Lorretta's son hadn't come for an unexpected visit. Then her body wouldn't have been found until after dinner at the earliest, right?"

"That's right, because she would have to miss two meals before anyone would check on her," Ruby agreed, propping her feet back on the thick slab of pine that was the top of her coffee table.

"And that would be the longest time she could be dead without being missed?"

"Unless she was killed immediately after putting out her beads at night. Then she wouldn't be checked until 9 a.m."

"If whoever poisoned her put it in the cinnamon–sugar shaker after her breakfast Friday, they might not have known about her family visiting. They might have expected the body not to be found until seven or eight Saturday night," Lucia mused.

"Did you know she ate cinnamon toast in the mornings? Was it common knowledge?" Amy asked. She slipped her Birkenstock sandals off and rested her feet on the coffee table too. Ruby flashed her a big grin before answering.

"Everybody knew exactly what Lorretta had for breakfast. She had a fit when the breakfast price went up. Told everyone what a cheat it was to charge three dollars for 'one slice of cinnamon toast, one half of a red grapefruit, and one cup of black coffee.' Frankly, we were all quite bored with hearing about her breakfast. I, for one, was quite grateful that she ate it by herself since she seemed to be prompted to her harangue by every meal."

"Did she also talk about her sugar shaker?" Lucia asked.

"Yep. How it came through the Straits of Magellan was a favorite story of hers. I don't think her own family was very well off. She never talked about them, just about her husband's family. I never thought of Lorretta as a talkative woman, but now that I look back on it, she was very open with people. Isn't that strange? Death does sometimes clarify one's impression of a person." Ruby tugged on a lock of hair right above her ear and managed to look charmingly pensive.

"Do you know anything about her finances?" Lucia asked, faithfully taking notes.

"Not much. She was obviously quite wealthy, even by the standards of this retirement center, where there are no poor and few even of the middle class. She did mention once that she had disinherited a son of hers for cowardice. Something about Vietnam, I believe. I don't recall anything else. She was president of a bank in Oklahoma."

"Who do you think killed her?" Amy asked.

"Certainly not Maggie. And I didn't. But I have no idea in the world who might have. She was often an irritating woman, but we'd have no population problem if people got killed merely for being irritating. In all my years on the *Carlsbad Chronicle*, I never once heard of a person getting killed just for being irritating. I'm afraid I didn't know Lorretta well enough to even have a suspicion." She watched Lucia writing furiously. "I think you need to give your hand a rest, Lucia. And I have to know. How is Maggie doing? Is there anything I can do to help? When will she be getting out of jail? Please tell me what's going on."

"I'm sorry, Ruby," Amy said. "It was insensitive to make you ask. You have every right to know." She explained what she had learned from the lawyer and what she and Lucia had gleaned from the Millett family. She continued, "Aunt Meg is doing as well as can be expected. She was very frantic when we saw her Monday afternoon but much calmer this morning. I don't understand why she didn't ask us to talk to you."

"She's trying to protect me. She made me promise I wouldn't get involved."

A bell rang in the kitchen, breaking the somber mood. "The water's ready for the pasta. Dinner in a moment, girls."

The conversation moved to lighter topics until dinner was finished. Ruby set a pot of hot water in the middle of the table and offered a small basket with an assortment of tea and coffee bags. "Let's talk about something else. The weather, perhaps."

Lucia grimaced. "Let's pick something less depressing than that."

"How about your coming out story?" Amy asked, wiggling her toes. "Do you mind sharing that?"

"Coming out," Ruby said. "For me that will always be the day I told my mother I was a lesbian. It took me many years to get enough courage. I was afraid to tell her when I fell in love with my college roommate or when that relationship ended. I couldn't talk about it when I met the woman I would spend the next ten years of my life with.

"I made excuses for not coming home for holidays. I was in terror that if my mother knew, her rigid Catholic faith would make her reject me. We grew further and further apart. Then my lover dumped me. I was devastated. I went home. One evening, my mother found me weeping, a sound she had not heard in twenty years. She asked what was wrong.

"'Cathy doesn't love me anymore,' I managed to say. My mother was wonderful. She hugged me and offered to go back to Albuquerque with me to take care of me.

"'I wish I could have told you earlier, but I didn't think you could deal with it,' I said to her. There was this long pause. It scared me to death. Then my mother responded, 'I think you may be right, but remember, parents grow too.' I've never forgotten that. She was a wonderful woman, my mother." A small tear slipped down Ruby's soft cheek.

"What a lovely story!" Amy exclaimed.

"But sad to have lost all those years of closeness while you waited for your mother to grow," Lucia commented.

"And your mother?" Ruby asked. "It wasn't any problem to tell her?"

"She died of tuberculosis of the bone when I was five. But if she had lived, I think it would have been very hard. Our family was Catholic, like yours, and very traditional. I'm not sure she ever could have accepted it. Perhaps her death was a kindness."

"I don't believe that for a minute, Lucia. There is no kindness in a five-year-old losing her mother," Amy broke in.

"Still, it would have hurt her. It seems so awful for love to bring pain." Lucia fished her tea bag out of her mug.

"Now you sound like Maggie," Ruby responded. "Sometimes it seems to me that she's afraid that her love is dangerous, that it will destroy anybody she loves." In the silence that followed, Lucia caught Amy's eye and gave a single pointed nod.

Amy's face flushed. "I can understand that. It's a problem I share with her."

"Probably something that polecat of a man did to you both. I don't know what rock that man crawled out from under at birth, but I wish he had crawled right back in. Looking at his life gives me a perverse appreciation of infanticide. Pardon me for talking about your father this way, but I believe I'm justified." Ruby looked at Amy fiercely, as if daring her to disagree.

"Then you know," Amy stated flatly.

"That your father committed incestuous rape on both his sister and daughter when they were too young to defend themselves? Yes, I do." The vehemence had not left Ruby's voice.

"I'm surprised Aunt Meg told you. She's always so close-mouthed about personal things," Amy replied.

"She didn't tell me. I told her. I had observed a terror in her response when the topics of men and sex intersected. That's not a normal response."

"Even for lesbians?" Amy asked.

"Even for lesbians, dear. Just because somebody doesn't like spinach and doesn't want to eat it, doesn't mean she's afraid of it. Of course, she might get irritated if people try to force her to eat spinach, but that still isn't fear. Fear always has a root cause. I just followed the path of Maggie's fear back to her brother." There was a grim satisfaction in Ruby's voice.

"And she told you about me?" Amy asked. "It's perfectly all right if she did. I've told her a hundred times that I don't want it to be a secret."

"Yes, she told me. She considers her failure to protect you from him one of the greatest failures of her life. Some days the shame and guilt of it consumes her. I have no way of consoling her. She is so full of regret for that, Amy. I wish there were some way she could make it up to you. She can't even talk to you about how she feels, she's so afraid you'll end up hating her. You are as close to a daughter as she will ever have. And she failed you, Amy. That failure is burned into her heart."

"This is terrible! I don't want her to feel that way. She was the only person who loved me and ..."

"And she left you in the clutches of a vicious rapist without lifting a finger to save you. That's how she views it," Ruby stated flatly.

"And what the hell could she do?" Amy shouted. "No one believed her when she told about her own rapes. They just locked her up in an institution and gave her shock treatments. Why would they believe her any more about me than they would have about herself?" Tears were streaming down Amy's face. She did not brush them away. The dampness left large dark spots on her blouse.

"She could have taken you and run away," Ruby continued inexorably, ignoring Amy's tears.

"And lived on what? Air? Kidnapping is a federal offense. There was no network to help women trying to protect their abused children then. It's hard to use a law degree to support a child when you are a felon fleeing the FBI. I can see the headlines now: Deranged Aunt Steals Child. My Aunt Meg wasn't stupid. There wasn't anything at all she could have done to save me. All of her choices would have just made the situation worse. He would have kept her from me, and she was the only safety I had."

"She could have at least confronted him. Told him to stop." Ruby's voice was cold.

"She came close one night. They both knew what she was talking about, although no one else at the dinner party did. The next morning he wrapped a hand towel around his fist and beat me very thoroughly before he went to work." Amy's voice became flat. Lucia put her arms around Amy and held her close. "Then he raped me. Then he choked me until I passed out. When I regained consciousness, he held my eyelids open and brought a lit cigarette close to each eye. He raped me again. Then he put a ten dollar bill up my vagina and told me to go see Aunt Meg. I took the money out and called a cab. I was in terrible pain. She took me to see a woman doctor she knew of. We gave false names. I had two broken ribs but not a mark on my body anywhere. The doctor taped up my ribs, and we never talked about it. The next time he might kill me. It was clear. So I ask, what could she have done? He held all the power. It took her years to manipulate a situation where he had to let me go away to college at least. I owe her my life and my sanity, such as it is. I don't appreciate hearing this kind of vicious, judgmental stand from someone who claims to be her lover."

Lucia caressed Amy's hair. "Querida, querida, you never told me about this." She kissed Amy's head gently. "I don't think Ruby is accusing Meg. She's just trying to tell you how Meg feels she's failed you."

"Is that right?" Amy asked, her voice broken with sobs.

Ruby nodded. "This anger at herself is eating my sweet Maggie up from the inside. It has to stop. I haven't been able to make her see sweet reason. I hoped to make you hear the voice she hears inside, judging herself. It must stop if Maggie is ever going to find happiness with herself, much less with me. I hope to enlist your help in silencing that voice of hatred inside herself. But first I had to know how you really felt, whether or not you considered her behavior moral cowardice, as she does. Heaven knows, I certainly don't want to make the situation worse."

"It was a brutal way to find that out," Amy said, wiping away her tears.

"I'm sorry for that, but I needed more information than polite lies provide. If I asked you if you blamed your aunt for not protecting you, you very well might have said, 'Of course not,' when you really did blame her. Anger is usually a way to short-circuit politeness. I'm sorry I didn't feel I had time for more finesse, but I'm desperately worried about Maggie. When I edited the paper, I saw several people confess to crimes they didn't commit to get the punishment they felt they deserved for other failures. Don't let that thought even cross Maggie's mind, please." Ruby seemed exhausted by the passion of the evening.

"I don't think Meg is going to confess, Ruby," Lucia responded, still stroking Amy's hair. "I have to ask, why do you call her Maggie instead of Meg? I hope I'm not prying."

Ruby smiled sadly. "We're beyond the concept of prying, I think. I don't call her Meg because that's what her brother called her."

Amy flinched inside the protection of Lucia's arms. Lucia hugged her. "I think we should go now. Can we talk to you again tomorrow?"

"Please do. And tell Maggie I would like her to stay with me when she gets out of jail. Then you girls can keep using her apartment, and I won't lose my mind with worry. I hold my promises very seriously, so I can't get involved directly with your investigation, but I very much want to help."

"Thank you, I think," Amy said. "I don't appreciate being attacked that way. Please don't ever do that to me again. It feels very unfair to me, and it was horribly unpleasant."

Ruby stood with them. "I'm sorry. Can you forgive a terrified old dyke for her lack of imagination?" She held her arms open.

Amy nodded her forgiveness and accepted an embrace from Ruby. After a moment, she returned the hug.

Lucia and Amy walked slowly back to Meg's apartment without speaking. Amy unlocked the door and let them both in. After she had closed and bolted the door, she went into the bedroom and undressed.

Lucia followed her, sitting on the edge of her single bed. "Do you want to talk about it?"

"Not yet. It's still too raw." Amy slipped off her slacks and folded them. She put them in the canvas bag she had brought for her dirty clothes.

"Okay. How about discussing information from the interviews? There are some things I think you might clarify." Lucia kicked off her shoes and stretched out on the bed.

"After my shower." Amy took off the rest of her clothes, folded them and walked naked into the small bathroom.

WEDNESDAY

Lucia gave up trying to find a tree to park under that was relatively close to the white clapboard building that housed the library. A neatly lettered sign on Village Circle Drive announced, "Mt. Vernon Subscription Library. Hours: Monday–Friday 2 p.m. to 5 p.m. Saturday 10 a.m. to 3 p.m." A "closed" sign was stuck in the window next to the door. Lucia and Amy followed the concrete path around to the back door of the house and knocked.

The door opened almost immediately. "Good, you're prompt," said the thin, attractive brunette at the door. "I'm Susan Bingham. Please come in."

Lucia looked quizzically at Amy. Ms. Bingham seemed more suited to New England than southern Alabama. "Thank you," Amy said. "We appreciate your meeting us this early. We didn't realize what the library hours were. Oh, by the way, I'm Amy Traeger." She extended her hand for a firm handshake as they entered the house.

"Lucia Ramos," Lucia said, also shaking the librarian's hand. They were in the kitchen of the small house, which apparently hadn't been remodeled since the fifties. Spotless white enamel cabinets covered three of the four walls. A table surfaced in mottled brown Formica stood on metal legs in the center of the small room. Susan pulled out one of the metal chairs that surrounded the table and sat primly on its brown upholstered seat. "Have a seat. Isn't it perfectly awful? I bought the house from a woman in her mid-eighties, a widow woman, as they say around here."

"You're not from here?" Amy asked as she and Lucia sat.

"No. I was a research librarian at MIT before I was diagnosed with chronic fatigue syndrome. Now I'm on total disability. That's why the hours of the library are so short. Saturdays, a high school girl keeps it open."

"That was quite of change of climate, psychic as well as physical," Amy commented.

"Quite true. But Alabama is a state where a small income stretches. I was quite firm that I wanted to be within thirty miles of Mobile as I rather enjoy the ambiance there, although there are few decent bookstores. I miss those the most. It's not difficult to buy a Bible in Mobile, but anything other than Christian literature is more of a challenge."

"Speaking of books," Lucia said, "you mentioned on the phone that you had helped Lorretta Millett track down some books."

"We were curious about the incredible variety of books in her apartment and hoped you might help us try to determine if any of them had something to do with her death," Amy added, putting her fingertips on the cool, slick surface of the Formica table. She leaned forward in her chair.

"Oh, I can't imagine any of them had anything to do with her being poisoned. Many of them were just the result of a bit of a game the two of us played." Susan paused for a moment to read the puzzled expression on Lucia's and Amy's faces. "We would do little research projects together. She'd been a librarian in her youth. One day when we were talking, the conversation drifted to the hardest research we'd ever done. Lorretta was convinced she could come up with a topic I couldn't find a book on. That's how this little contest began. It amused us both immensely."

"So that's why she had a book about the 1936 Olympics," Lucia said.

"Yes, I suppose. There were times when I wasn't sure she was just playing a game. She was a very complex woman." She paused. "Frankly, it makes me a bit uncomfortable to talk about this. It's as close as I've ever come to being unethical about the confidentiality of patron usage."

"I'm sorry," Amy rushed to say. "I'm a therapist. I've great respect for confidentiality. We don't want to put you in an unethical position."

"I thought about it all evening after your call. Lorretta and I did this research as friends and she's dead now. I don't mind sharing my records. I've decided that the issue of confidentiality is irrelevant in this instance. I doubt if I could help clear your aunt, but Margaret Traeger is one of my favorite patrons, so I pulled together the records that I have." She spread several sheets of paper out on the table. "These books weren't in the library, of course. I have an arrangement with a friend at Auburn. She gets the requested books through interlibrary loan and ships them UPS."

Lucia checked off all the titles that had been listed in the police report. Then she added the new titles to her notebook. "Guinness Book of Olympic Records?" she questioned.

"Yes, Lorretta was very interested in the 1936 Winter Olympics. We started with the Guinness book, but it didn't seem to answer whatever question she was researching. It took quite a bit of research to turn up the other book, *Striving*. I don't know if it had the information she wanted. It only came in on Tuesday."

"Did you read it?" Lucia asked.

"I've read every book in this small library, and I haven't the funds for many new ones. My tastes and my subscribers' tastes are not a good match. They are surprisingly interested in Shakespeare. My college text with all his plays is my single most popular title. Rosamunde Pilcher is a more popular author, though. The men like Zane Grey."

"Did you read the financial books?" Lucia asked.

"No. Not really to my taste. I did enjoy Ante-Bellum Mansions of Alabama. We were trying to research Heritage Farms, which was supposedly built in 1854. It wasn't.

Turns out it was built in 1926 by a rumrunner named Albert Chestang, whose family still lives up in Calvert. He amassed quite a fortune by his efforts and spent much of it on conspicuous consumption. The Main House was badly damaged by a hurricane in the early thirties, and by that time he had lost so much money in the crash that he couldn't afford to fix it. He donated it to the Presbyterian church, although why that particular branch of Christianity seems a bit of a mystery, since he and his entire family were Methodists. Perhaps he didn't want to saddle his own church with the upkeep. At any rate, I found the rendition of the story in Gracious Houses of the Gulf Coast most amazing."

"I wonder where the books are? They weren't listed as being in the evidence room, so the police don't still have them. I guess they're still in Lorretta's apartment," Lucia said.

"No, as a matter of fact, her son brought them by yesterday. They're still in a box. I haven't had the energy to unpack them." Susan gestured toward the main part of the house.

"Could we borrow them?" Amy asked excitedly.

"Of course. Do you mind getting them? The box is next to my desk right through the door."

Lucia was back in moment with a cardboard box full of the books.

"I regret that I must draw this conversation to a close. I need to conserve my energy so that I can open the library this afternoon. I hope you'll forgive my abruptness. Please feel free to call if there is anything else I can help you with. I genuinely like your aunt, Amy. I hope this mess is quickly resolved in her favor."

They shook hands over the table. Lucia and Amy showed themselves to the door.

"Ruby wants to help. Why don't we ask her to go through these books?" Amy suggested. "She knows the situation at Heritage House much better than we do. With her background in journalism, I think we could count on her investigative abilities."

"Good idea, Traeger. I'll make a cop of you yet. Passing off work to people you can count on is an important part of good police work."

"Laziness, you mean," Amy laughed.

"Yep. But never call it that. Call it delegation."

The drive to Red Fox Lane was several miles. The houses in this neighborhood were not well kept up. Many had peeling paint and several had lawns with tall grass. Lucia gestured at one. "They'd better know that they're going to get snakes in the house."

"Is that why people mow?" Amy asked with the innocence of her urban childhood.

"Mostly. Tall grass or weeds hide snakes, mosquitoes, all sorts of unpleasant surprises," she said, parking in front of the sign that proclaimed "Kay's Kuts and Kurls."

They followed a cheery path of concrete stepping stones, set in a bed of short pansies, that led to the back of the garage. An old tool shed had been gutted and plumbed and made over into a charming, if small, beauty salon.

The door was opened before either could knock. A sturdy woman with thick, greying hair answered the door. Her manner was very lively. She stuck her hand out. "Hi, I'm Kay Newbolt. I heard you drive up. Not many cars take this street this time of day."

Amy shook her hand and was impressed with its strength. "I'm Amy Traeger and this is my colleague Lucia Ramos. I want to thank you for agreeing to this interview."

"Well, I don't see any reason not to talk to you. I felt real sorry when Miz Millett died. She was a regular. Every Friday, just like clockwork. She paid well. They all did at the Home. Well enough I could pay the referral fee, my gas, my lost time for the drive and still come out ahead. Would one of you like a shampoo? On the house? I just feel more comfortable talking when my hands are busy."

Amy and Lucia looked at each other. Amy shrugged and said, "I could use a shampoo. But I don't mind paying for it, I really don't."

"Well, I'll take your money then. I surely can use it. My ex is about as regular with his child support as an old-timer with his colon sewed up. Just nothing comes out at all." Both Lucia and Amy smiled while Kay busied herself with her equipment.

"Did you have regular appointments with any other residents?" Lucia asked.

"Yep. I had almost a dozen. Miz Brown, Miz Fletcher, she's not one of the old-timers, but she lives out there because her husband is the sales manager for the Home. He's a nasty bit of work, a real snake-oil salesman. I do them on Tuesday, then on Wednesday I do Miz Abbot and Miz Malone. They live across from each other on what I call the bridge wing because all my girls on that wing play bridge together.

"Thursday I do Miz Worthington every week and Miz Dupre every other week. On Friday I do Miz Hoffman and Miz Millett every week and Miz Sewell every other week. They all want to look nice for bridge club in the afternoon, so I have to start real early in the morning to get them all in. Effie next door takes my little girl to school on Fridays. Well, this water is just about perfect, so you just sit down and relax, Miz Traeger." She gestured to the single sink with its brown Naugahyde recliner. Amy took the seat and leaned back into the niche scalloped for necks. She relaxed into Kay's strong fingers.

"That's nine appointments," Lucia said.

"Yep. Those are my shampoo ladies. Then I have two more that I cut once a month. Your Aunt and Miz Mazioli. I regret to say that some of the other ladies refer to her as Mazola Oil, and I have to say that there's some justice in that name." Kay worked a generous dab of apple-scented shampoo into Amy's honey-brown hair. "She is one who could use a weekly shampoo. Or daily. Not like your aunt. Her hair is always squeaky clean when I go to cut it. Does she shampoo it before I get there?" Kay asked, massaging Amy's scalp through the shampoo.

"Probably," Amy murmured, not wanting to break her relaxation with too much thought.

"Did any of your customers talk about Mrs. Millett?" Lucia asked, still writing notes on the last bit of Kay's conversation.

"Yep, they did. Not much to do but gossip out there. Not like they still had a house full of kids to keep them hopping. I can't say there was a lot of kindness in their talk about Miz Millett. She was not a woman who inspired kindness, if you know what I mean." Her fingers tightened momentarily on Amy's scalp.

"But you kept her as a customer?" Lucia asked.

"Well, in case you haven't noticed, Mt. Vernon, Alabama, has a tad fewer people than New York City. And I'm not the only beautician. If I start getting choosy about my customers, I'll be on welfare pretty quick. I'm just real lucky those little old ladies like me or I'd have a tough time making it." Kay gently rinsed out the shampoo and put on an apple-scented conditioner.

"You could move to Mobile," Amy suggested.

"Or New York City. And have my baby girl in school with crack sellers and murderers. No, thank you. I know every vice in Mt. Vernon. I'm used to them. I know that I can't protect my baby from all of them, but at least I know what I'm up against." Kay stuck a damp towel in the microwave and set it for sixty seconds.

"Better the devil you know than the devil you don't know," Amy said from her almost-prone position.

"Yep. That's not to say I couldn't get used to a big city. I reckon people can get used to anything. Why, I could get used to being hung by the neck if I did it long enough." Kay was distracted from the rest of her thoughts by the bell on the microwave. She removed the warmed towel and instructed Amy to sit up. "We'll just wrap this around that conditioner to help it soak in. It just takes a few minutes."

"Did you ever notice any books around Mrs. Millett's apartment?" Lucia asked.

"She had some. Not nearly as many as Miz Sewell or your aunt. Between them I think they carried an entire public library to that home. They sure are readers, always talking about books. Made me wish I had the time to read some of them. Your aunt loaned me one; it had a funny title but it surely was good reading. Bean Trees. That was it, Bean Trees. I really liked that book, but it took me nigh on to six months to finish it. But Miz Millett, she never talked much at all, and, for sure, she didn't talk about books." Kay unwrapped Amy's head and laid it back in the wash bowl for rinsing.

"You blow-dry your hair?" Kay asked her.

"Usually."

"Okay," she said, plugging in a plum-colored plastic blowdryer. She warmed it up, then put her hand in front of it to be sure it wasn't too hot.

"Were you surprised when she was murdered?" Lucia asked.

"I surely was. I kind of expect to lose some of those old ladies to age, but poison? I've never known anybody who was poisoned. Course, maybe I did and just didn't know it was poison. Like at first they thought it was her heart, and then her daughter-in-law made them do that autopsy and they found poison. No telling how many murders they'd discover if they autopsied every dead body around here. Take that wretched Clyde Cunningham, the way he keeled over, it could have been Emma knocking him off for all the years he knocked her around. Course, alcohol is poison if you drink enough of it, and Clyde surely did that."

"Do you know anybody who might have wanted to kill

her? Did she ever talk about having enemies?" Amy asked.

"She was a closemouthed one, she was. Mostly she would ask me questions."

"Such as?" Lucia queried.

"How long I lived here. Had I ever been inside the Main House at Heritage Farms?"

"Heritage Farms? Not Heritage House?" Amy clarified.

"That's right. The plantation goes back before the War Between the States." Lucia and Amy exchanged glances but said nothing. "They built Heritage House only about five years ago. The director, he lives at the Main House. I went through it once, when I was in high school. That's when the church owned it. They used it like some kind of retirement home for old ministers, I guess. It was a historic homes tour. For three dollars you got to see five big old houses in Citronelle, Heritage Farms, and the Boyd place up on Pitt Road. We were supposed to see the Rivers Estate in McIntosh, but they backed out at the last minute."

"So, as far as you know, Mrs. Millett didn't have any enemies?" Lucia probed again.

"Not as far as I know, but it wouldn't surprise me any. She didn't notice people. It was like she could stand on your big toe and never even notice you screaming." She finished brushing out Amy's hair and looked at Lucia.

"How about you? I could give you a quickie. I don't need to be up at the Home for another hour."

Lucia shrugged and took Amy's place in the chair.

"Could you tell us about the other members of the Friday bridge club?" Lucia asked, hoping Amy was taking notes.

"Well, there's Miz Abbot..."

"That's okay. She and Ms. Malone we don't need to know about, since they've been out of town the last week," Amy said.

"Well, how about my Thursday girl, Miz Worthington?"

"Yes," Lucia said. "We'd like to know about her."

"She's just crazy for fabrics. Every square inch of her wall is covered with cloth. She has some from just about every place under the sun. Some I never heard of until she told me about it. Namibia. I never heard of Namibia until she told me. It's inside South Africa. This church started a weaving co-op called Women Hold Up the Sky. Isn't that a nice name? Now there's poetry for you. Well, Miz Worthington hasn't been herself since her roommate got sick and died, about a year ago. She used to be a sight more chipper than she is now. I think she broke her ankle because she just flat didn't care. Before her friend died, she used to copy all these funny things and stick them on bulletin boards, like the 1040EZ tax form. It only had two lines. The first one said, 'How much money do you have?' The second line said, 'Send it all to the IRS.'

"Her sense of humor is coming back, though. Last wash, she asks me, 'Do you know why pigs can't fly?' When I said, 'No,' she said, 'Because they weren't President Bush's Chief of Staff.' I laughed pretty good. I'm not sure, though, that John Sinununum, or whatever his name was, wasn't a pig in disguise. He surely liked stuffing himself at the taxpayers' trough, now, didn't he?"

"Yes. Did she like Mrs. Millett?" Amy asked.

"She never said anything against her. Now, Miz Hoffman, she never said a nice word about Miz Millett. They were having a tug of war over that deaf piano player, Earl Banks. I don't know why either one of them wanted him. He didn't sound much better than Clyde Cunningham to me. From what I hear he drinks too much, gets mad a lot, and only wants their money. But I never met the man, so who am I to judge?"

"So Mrs. Hoffman had a grudge against Mrs. Millett," Lucia prompted from the wash basin.

"Seems like it to me. Those ladies were talking about it all the time, especially Miz Malone, who said he'd probably forgotten what to do with it even if the miracle occurred and he could get it up. She has a point. I know from my own scum of an ex-husband that drinkers have a real hard time performing the marriage act. But that didn't keep those two old dogs from fighting over him like he was a bone. Miz Millett, I'm not sure she really cared for him, but she had him first and hated to give up anything that she considered hers." She wrapped Lucia's head in the warm towel.

"Now, this is not right. I'm going to give you ladies the idea that she was a skinflint and a cheat, which she was not. She never balked over the thirty-five dollar price. Not like that Mrs. Fletcher. Oh, she's a weasel, that one. All my other girls give me a check. Not her. Every Tuesday she tries to give me a twenty dollar bill. 'Oh, I only have two twenties,' she says in that sorority girl voice of hers. 'I can't imagine you carry change. Why don't we just let it be twenty this week?'" Both Lucia and Amy smiled at the satire of her mimicry.

"What about Ruby Sewell?" Amy asked.

"Pure gold, that one. She always gives me a five-dollar tip. She appreciates the work and knows how to make that clear. She's a talker, that one. I just love her stories about her newspaper. Boy, they certainly had a lot of murders in Carlsbad, New Mexico. I guess it being a frontier town and all."

"Did she get along with Mrs. Millett?" Lucia asked as Kay began to blow-dry her hair.

"I guess so. She never talked about any problems. She doesn't talk much about people in the present. Mostly she talks about New Mexico. I think she misses it a lot. Says her skin is much better here, though. More moisture." Kay gave Lucia's hair one last flip with the brush.

"We're going to have to leave now if I'm going to have time to take you back to Heritage House for your interview with the maid and still make Aunt Meg's hearing," Amy said.

"Don't you worry about that. I'll just carry her over to

the home myself, if you want," Kay said, straightening out her sink area.

"Thank you. That would be a help," Amy said, signing two twenty-dollar traveler's checks. "Is that okay with you, Lucia?"

"No problem," Lucia replied. "It'll give you a little more time with Meg. Thank you for the offer, Kay. I appreciate it."

Kay packed up two overnight cases with her supplies and picked up a plastic bag with folded towels in it.

"Could I help carry something?" Lucia asked.

"Sure, you can pick up those cases." She shooed Lucia and Amy out the door and locked it. "Didn't used to have to lock but things are changing even in Mt. Vernon, Alabama. I guess crime is everywhere."

She backed a metallic blue Geo from the rickety garage while Lucia and Amy said goodbye. She reached across and unlocked the passenger door for Lucia. "Just throw those cases in the back seat, honey." Kay pulled out from her gravel driveway onto the decaying pavement of Red Fox Road.

"I'm curious, Kay. You said you do Ms. Abbott and Ms. Malone on Wednesdays. How come you're going over there if they're both on a cruise?"

Kay giggled. "You caught me on that one, honey. I'll tell you, but don't you be telling anyone else or it's my job. I do Mr. Fletcher's hair. I have to be real discreet about it since he thinks he runs the place. You know how some men don't want anyone to know they're having their hair styled instead of just going to a barber? Well, he's one of them." She giggled again. "I give him exactly the same cut as Ruby Sewell and nobody has ever noticed. Now isn't that a kick and a half?" she said, swinging the car onto U.S. 45.

"Yeah, it is. Another thing I noticed was that the prices in the shop are different than what you charge the residents of Heritage House."

"Not really," Kay said a little defensively. "They're both

twenty dollars. Let's see, I charge twenty dollars for the shampoo; then there is the fifteen-dollar delivery fee. I pay fifteen percent back to the office."

"Fifteen percent?" Lucia questioned, amazed.

"Sure. They don't let just any riffraff in to Heritage House to work their tomfoolery with the residents. You get checked out and then you sign a contract as long as your arm that boils down to agreeing that you won't steal from the residents, you won't sell any stories to the newspaper, and you won't bad-mouth the management. Plus you got to figure I'm using their hot water. Five and a quarter is fine by me.

"Then there's the four percent tax to the state, that takes another dollar forty. That leaves me just under thirty dollars. It takes me about the same amount of time driving out to the home as it does to do a shampoo, plus I've got to put gas in the car." She patted the fake-fur-trimmed dash. "So I figure I'm in the hole if I only do one appointment. Fridays are best when I have three, four, sometimes five in a row. I'm sure going to miss Miz Millett," she said.

Her speed began to creep up. She swerved to avoid an elderly black man who was inching his equally elderly Chevy out of his driveway and onto the highway.

"If you don't mind, Kay, can you not do that again until I'm out of this car." Lucia swallowed to relax her throat muscles.

"Why, honey, I'm sorry. I thought being a cop and all you'd be used to that kind of driving." She took her foot off the gas pedal, and the car slowed to within ten miles of the speed limit.

"I mostly worked juvenile, not traffic. Besides, if I'm in a car traveling at that rate of speed, I'm usually driving." Lucia let out a slow sigh of relief.

"Yezzir, those trust issues are killers, aren't they?"

"Excuse me?" Lucia was totally lost.

Kay rested her tanned elbow on the window ledge. She

held the steering wheel with one hand and used the other to fiddle with the buttons on the car radio.

"My ex-husband and I went to a lot of marriage encounter weekends trying to fix things up before we finally separated. They were always having us work on trust issues. It really helped me realize that I didn't trust that SOB. I would never do the exercises once we got home. I knew Dane would always catch me if people were watching, but at home alone...Why, that polecat would just as soon let me drop as go whoring. Fat chance I'd fall backwards into those arms. Only reason he wants the kids is that people expect him to. Oh, and to make me hurt for embarrassing him. Yep, it's all trust issues." She slapped the steering wheel for vehemence. For a moment there were no hands on the steering wheel.

"I think it might be a good idea to let me off before we get to Heritage House. I've got lots of time before my noon appointment, and I don't want you to get into trouble for helping me. We're not exactly favorites of Mr. Fletcher."

"I know. I got an earful from Mrs. Fletcher during yesterday's shampoo."

Kay tapped the rhythm from "Your Cheatin' Heart" on the steering wheel while an unfamiliar voice sang it to the airwaves.

"What did she say?" Lucia asked.

"She says they're going to have to raise the rates again at Heritage House. Her husband said a bunch of new government regulations are going to be real expensive. Then on top of that some 'deranged old dyke'—excuse me, but that's what she said—goes and poisons a rich old lady. They don't like you two stirring things up. Seems like that place is just like a hornet's nest with people whizzing around looking for someone to sting."

She stopped the car abruptly. "There's a bridle path from here to the House. It cuts over from the Farms. It's only about three-quarters of a mile. The horses keep the snakes away so it should be clear. You mind walking from here?"

Lucia checked her watch. "No, I've got plenty of time. Thanks for the lift, Kay."

"Pure pleasure. I want that sweet Margaret Traeger out of jail. After all, I can't afford to lose another customer." She waved as she gunned the engine. Two black marks were laid down on the grey highway by the tires.

Lucia shook her head and started down the path. It seemed fairly well maintained. Bushes were trimmed back about four feet from the center of the trail. Old marks of horseshoes deeply indenting wet earth had been pounded almost smooth by traffic on drier days. She recognized few of the shrubs or trees. They didn't look anything like the hackberry, mesquite, and cane scrub she had grown up with along the Rio Grande. Only the oak was familiar. There were several examples of a white flowering bush that she wished she could identify. The subtle, sweet perfume was a delight. She picked a blossom and breathed its scent in deeply while she walked briskly down the bridle path.

Within ten minutes she was approaching the back door of Heritage House that was closest to Meg's apartment. She withdrew the key from her slacks pocket and opened the heavy metal door. There was no one inside to see her. She hurried into the apartment. The fewer people who knew she was there, the less likely Ruth Hanckel was to get in trouble for talking to her.

The apartment seemed very empty. Lucia felt almost like an intruder without Amy to validate her presence. She took a quick shower to wash off the sweat and dust from her walk. At this rate she'd need to do laundry soon. Two changes a day was stretching her limited wardrobe to the breaking point.

She had just settled at the dining room table with her case notes when a light knock at the door drew her to her feet. "Coming," she called toward the door. She opened it to a young woman dressed in an aqua-colored slacks uniform. Her long black hair was in a French braid. Her dark brown eyes considered Lucia very carefully. Their skin tones were an exact match of brown, but Lucia's cheekbones were not as high nor as prominent.

"Please come in. I'm Lucia Ramos. Amy Traeger, Meg's niece, is in Citronelle at the arraignment. I hope you don't mind."

Ruth entered, pulling her metal cart full of cleaning supplies behind her, which she parked in the small kitchen. She brought a brown paper bag of lunch to the table with her.

"It's fine," she said, showing Lucia the bag. "But I have to eat lunch while we talk. This is my only break."

"Sure. Do you mind if I tape our talk?" Lucia asked.

"Fine," Ruth replied, keeping her eyes on Lucia as they both sat. Lucia turned on the tape recorder.

"How long have you worked at Heritage House?" she asked.

"About three months." She paused and seemed to make a decision. "Believe it or not, I'm here working on my master's thesis." Lucia had no trouble believing that those dark intelligent eyes fed a mind pursuing an advanced degree.

"What in? It can't be in cleaning rooms for a retirement complex."

Ruth snorted. "No, you're right. It's in anthropology. I found a way to earn academic credit 'studying' myself."

"I don't think that I understand," Lucia said, bemused.

"Sorry. I thought you were Native American," Ruth apologized. "Your eyes, your skin, your hair. I just assumed you were from a tribe."

"I probably am, in large part. My family is mestizo from near Guanajuato in Mexico. I have both Spanish and Indian blood." Lucia was intrigued with the direction of the conversation. She decided to put investigation of the murder on the back burner for a while. "But you're full-blooded Indian?"

"Probably not. But all my recorded ancestors were Apache. That's why I'm here."

"I didn't know this was Apache territory. I thought it's where all the Oklahoma Indians came from. The Cherokees, the Choctaws, the Chickasaws, the Creeks. They were all forced out on the Trail of Tears."

"You're right. The Apache I'm studying didn't live here by choice. They were the last survivors of the Warm Springs Apache, led by Geronimo."

"What on earth were they doing in Mt. Vernon, Alabama?" Lucia asked.

"What good Indians do best, dying. They were originally sent to Florida to die, but too much attention was focused on them there. So they moved the tribe here, or actually to the swamps up by what is now the state hospital. I'm studying the remains of their camp." Ruth stopped talking and took another bite of her sandwich. They sat quietly for a while.

Then Lucia said, "I guess a lot of them died here."

"Most of them. TB, yellow fever, malaria. They were all terribly malnourished. They'd been raised on the foods of the Southwest. They didn't know what was edible in this jungle on the Gulf coast. They had no weapons to hunt with. The government swore in its treaty to feed them, but it lied. I have read report after report praising the success of the extermination program. The Army was quite proud of itself." She paused again to eat.

"There was one doctor with a conscience, Walter Reed. He repeatedly asked for more provisions, especially salt. It's very important here, where people sweat so much in the summer. Finally he gave up and asked for a transfer. No one would let him help."

"And no one else wanted to?" Lucia asked.

"They had embarrassed the army. Fewer than fifty

Apache warriors were chased by over five thousand soldiers for years. It was humiliating. So they wanted all the Warm Springs Apache dead. They were very successful. Almost all the children died. The few that survived were sent away.

"When my great-grandfather was a prisoner of war at eight, they sent him to school in Pennsylvania for three years. During the summers he and the other kids were sold as slave labor to local farmers. His owner was a very nice man named Detrich Hanckel, a Quaker. He gave my great-grandfather clothes and fed him very well. That's probably why he didn't die of disease like many of the other imprisoned children.

"My great-grandfather took this man's name as a sign of respect and kinship. He learned farming and animal husbandry from this man. When our tribe was repatriated, we were sent to live with the Mescalero tribe on their reservation. My family was given housing high on the mountain where the summers were very short. My great-grandfather tried farming, but after a while he just grew hay for the cattle's winter feed. So, you see, even my name is not my own."

Lucia nodded, thinking how little she knew of her own family history beyond her grandparents. And they were all dead now. There was no one to ask. "It seems like an important thing to study."

"I had to fight for it. Anthro was sure it was a history topic. White men are very proud of the fences they put around parts of wisdom. Nothing must ever cross the fence. I finally used the argument that it was a study of a transitional aboriginal group under extreme external stress. I was approved. I go out to the site every Sunday when I don't have to work." Ruth snapped off the tip of a whole carrot with her strong white teeth. She chewed carefully as if she really tasted the sweetness of the carrot.

"Do you clean for the entire wing?" Lucia directed the conversation back to the investigation.

"Except for the German couple across from Mrs. Millett. I only cleaned there once. She watched me like a hawk," she said, folding the waxed paper from her sandwich.

Lucia looked at Ruth quizzically.

"Not like I was going to steal something. A lot of the old ladies do that. They're very realistic about the effects of poverty. No, it was more like I was a bull in a china shop. She wouldn't let me near anything that might break. When I vacuumed she spent a long time showing me how the furniture had to go so it would be exactly where it had been before I moved it." Ruth tucked the waxed paper back inside the brown lunch sack and folded it also. "That was fairly strange. I'm very professional. Most of the women I clean for figure that out pretty quickly, and then they breathe a sigh of relief and leave me alone. But not her. She checked the label of every cleaner I used. She even told me exactly how she wanted the toilet cleaned. Very weird. Pathological about germs. I felt like I was scrubbing down a surgery room in a hospital." Ruth took another bite of carrot.

"Did she talk about Mrs. Millett at all?" Lucia asked.

There was a pause as Ruth chewed her carrot.

"I really don't remember. It was months ago. Sorry."

"Do any of the other people you clean for talk about her?"

"No. I don't really see them much. Once they realize I'm not a thief, they try to be out of the apartment when I clean. The vacuum makes a lot of noise, and some people aren't used to conversing with a maid so they just pretend I'm not there. That's okay with me." She bit off another piece of carrot and began to chew.

"When did you last clean Mrs. Millett's apartment?"

Ruth paused in her chewing. She looked at Lucia intently, then resumed chewing. After swallowing, she asked, "Can I trust you?"

"I'm not sure what you mean. If you tell me something

illegal, I'm bound by my oath to report it. I can't cover up or ignore information in a criminal case." Lucia sighed internally, knowing her answer would probably prevent any significant disclosure.

Ruth took a final bite of the carrot and chewed it thoughtfully, looking at Lucia's eyes the entire time.

"I could get fired for this, but it's not criminal. At least, I don't think it is. I would appreciate it if you didn't let it get back to the director. Jobs in Mt. Vernon are very hard to come by, especially when you don't have any friends or family here." She paused, staring at Lucia intently. "I went to clean Saturday morning."

Lucia raised her eyebrows but said nothing.

"She wanted me to clean after the bridge club but before her family came. It was extra money, but I'm not supposed to do it. It's against policy. But," she shrugged, "it was twenty extra bucks, so I agreed. I was about ten minutes late. I knocked. There wasn't an answer. I figured her family had come early and she was already gone, so I keyed the door with my master key. See, I did this every couple of months when she had bridge club. It's no big thing. I do it for Dorothy Hoffman too. Anyway, I opened the door and she was lying on the floor, dead. So I closed the door and left. If I called anyone, I'd be fired. And it was too late to help, so...." She shrugged.

"You were sure she was dead?" Lucia asked.

"Yeah. Where I grew up, kids saw dead people. We're not like the Navajos. They're very careful of the dead. They abandon a house if someone dies in it. I helped take care of both my grandparents when they were dying. Dead just looks dead. It's not hard to tell by looking. She was dead."

"So you just left the body and went home?"

Ruth looked a little sheepish. "No. I had asked Margaret Traeger and Minerva Worthington if I could switch their cleaning days from Monday to that Saturday. It was okay with them. That meant I didn't have to come in until 11 a.m. on Monday. I worked the switch so no one would be upset if they saw me in the building on Saturday. So I just went on and cleaned their apartments."

"Do you empty trash cans when you clean?"

"Sure. And clean the toilet, tub, and sinks. I vacuum, do a little light dusting, mop the kitchen floor. Check the oven and refrigerator for spills or grossities and I'm out of there. It usually takes about an hour to an hour and a half. Why?"

"Would you be willing to testify that you emptied Margaret Traeger's wastebasket from her bathroom on Saturday morning?" Lucia asked.

"Sure, since I had switched her day to Saturday, I was supposed to do that. I can't get in trouble for saying I did it. How come you want me to testify to that? It seems weird," she commented.

"Something was found in her wastebasket on Sunday night that the police feel implicated her. It might help that it wasn't in there on Saturday. Perhaps someone other than Meg put it there."

"Well, any of these old people could have gotten in. They all have keys to each other's apartments."

"And there are extra keys at the front desk. Who else might have a key, maybe a master if they got into both the Traeger and the Millett apartment?" Lucia asked.

"Anyone who works in health care. They have to be able to get in an apartment fast in an emergency. I don't think they even lock the key box where they all hang. I don't know who else. I have to go now. My lunch period is up. Good luck to Ms. Traeger." Ruth stood and extended her hand for a shake. "And good luck to you, Lucia. I hope some day you start learning more about your real culture."

Lucia shook hands firmly. "It was a real pleasure, Ruth. Good luck on your thesis. And thanks for talking to me. That trash emptying may be just what we need." Ruth grabbed her cart and left.

Lucia packed her notebook and recorder and hurried out the door for her appointment with Earl Banks. His door was equipped with a light switch labeled "Please switch on for entry." It seemed to Lucia like a good idea to have a light instead of a knocker in the apartment of a deaf resident. She flipped the switch up. When, after several minutes, no one answered the door, she flipped it up and down a few times. There was still no answer. After a few more minutes, Lucia decided to try knocking.

As she was rapping on the door, an arm went around her shoulders in a light embrace.

"It won't do a bit of good. I'm deaf as a post and besides I'm out here, not in there. Sorry to be late, Miss Ramos. I'm Earl Banks."

Lucia turned toward the elderly man, ignoring the arm he draped over her shoulder. He was attractive in an aging-movie-star way. His hair, which seemed natural, was thick and white. He was dressed casually in a lime golf shirt and cream slacks. His blue eyes twinkled.

Lucia used the American Sign Language she had learned volunteering at the Sunshine School for the Deaf to introduce herself as she made the same introduction out loud. Earl Banks paid no attention to either.

"I never bothered to learn sign language," he said. "You can't teach an old dog new tricks. Just write down anything you want to say and show it to me. It's cumbersome, but it works." He put an arm around her waist and escorted her into the apartment.

The living room was arranged like a miniature recital hall. A grand piano was placed in front of the sliding glass doors to the balcony. The well-kept lawn and trees provided a dramatic backdrop only slightly marred by the balcony railing. There was a five-foot space devoid of furniture, then two short rows of padded folding chairs.

"Do you mind if I play while we talk? I am much more relaxed while I commune with the muse of music." Lucia nodded her agreement.

He seated her in the front row and proceeded to the piano. Lucia suspected that performing before an audience, even of one, was closer to his goal than relaxation. She opened her briefcase on the maroon plush seat of the chair next to her and took out her notebook. She started to write a question as he began to play a Strauss waltz. Then she tore it up as he anticipated it with his monologue.

"My acquaintance with Lorretta was rocky. I found her stimulating but so mistrustful. She loved music. She was a significant donor to the Oklahoma City Chamber Music Festival. I am rarely taken seriously as a musician here at Heritage House. I'm viewed more like a talking dog. You can understand, I know, how much it means to a musician to be taken seriously. Especially since late in life he has been robbed of his hearing.

"But enough about me. Poor Lorretta. She never had the happy, warm, loving family she so desperately wanted. Her mother died of the flu in that terrible epidemic during World War I. Lorretta was only an infant, but her father, who was a doctor, deserted her to join the army. She never saw or heard from him again."

Lucia noticed that his voice occasionally took on the rhythm he was playing. She wondered if he was doing it with the unconscious beat he must feel to play at all, or whether Ruby was right and he could hear better than he seemed to.

"She was raised by her Grandmother Winn, who sent her to Normal School when she was fifteen. She had little aptitude for teaching but found a true home in the library. She was recommended to the librarian at Oklahoma State University, who gave her a position." He broke into a tango. Lucia smiled. He might be a gigolo, but he apparently had a sense of humor. "There she met Laurence, who became her sweetheart, then her fiancé, then her husband. At the height of the Depression she fell deeply in love with a still-wealthy man. They had a son, Larry Junior. Meanwhile, Larry Senior worked in his father's bank, loaning money only to those who didn't need it." He switched to a medley of George M. Cohan tunes.

"War again brought tragedy to Lorretta's life. While she was pregnant with her second son, her husband was killed in England. Lorretta abandoned their home and moved in with her husband's family. She began to work at their bank. Years later she was made vice president. But the Korean War drew her oldest son and he was killed on Hill 278." The medley of war songs ended. He moved into Beethoven.

"The death of his grandson broke the heart of the elderly Mr. Millett. He turned the bank over to his daughter-in-law and retired." The music crescendoed. "Lorretta found total fulfillment in the bank. Other than the cowardice and feck-lessness of her younger son, she was content. Never a woman to deny change, she realized when the era of family-owned banks passed. Oklahoma Farmers Bank and Trust was sold to First Interstate and Lorretta moved here..." Lucia wrote a note and walked over to put it on the music stand of the piano. Earl continued talking, "where she met me. Oh, yes, I do know why she selected Heritage House. She liked the inheritance laws in Alabama, and she was impressed that Heritage House had hired a former bank officer, Sam Pettigrew, as the director. The fact that he was an ex-priest was also reassuring, as Lorretta was raised Catholic, although she left the church after her marriage over the issue of birth control. I think she rather respected more the people who left the church than the ones who stayed in. Perhaps that explains her fascination with Sam Pettigrew." He read the next question Lucia had propped up.

"I cannot imagine anyone murdering anyone, much less Lorretta." Lucia took the note off and wrote a single word at the bottom.

"Dorothy? Don't be absurd. She's seventy-five years old. Crimes of passion are ill-suited to the elderly. We simply don't care that much anymore. I'd bet you a hundred dollars that Lorretta was murdered over money. Probably that ne'er-do-well son of hers or her grasping grandson. They are the ones who'll inherit." He seemed impatient with the interactiveness of the exchange. He began to play "Good Night, Irene."

"I find this has become tedious, Miss Ramos. If you will excuse me, I wish to nap," he said, rising and heading for the bedroom.

Lucia collected her notes off the piano and showed herself out. She went back to Meg's apartment to wait until her appointment with Dorothy Hoffman. She reviewed her notes from the interviews with Ruth Hanckel and Earl Banks. She wrote up reports for Amy to review. Neither had mentioned Meg as a suspect, but that could be mere politeness. She chewed the end of her black Papermate pen. Neither had added much to her understanding of the case, but Ruth's information about the wastebasket could be valuable. She underlined a phrase here and there, then checked her watch.

Dorothy Hoffman opened the door into a room of massive mahogany furniture, where blue upholstered wing chairs were dwarfed by a massive sideboard placed between them. The chairs were not designed for human anatomy, Lucia decided, after trying unsuccessfully to find a comfortable position. While Dorothy discussed the oppressive heat and humidity, Lucia studied her carefully. Her smile seemed fake. It didn't match the creases in her aging face.

Her long, thin, grey hair was pulled back severely into a knot with onyx clips holding it into place. The skin of her face had loosened to reveal the sharp edges of bone in her checks and brow and the tendons and veins ridging downward in her neck. Several layers of skin lay loosely at the base of her neck. They showed through the black collar of her red silk blouse patterned with a gold Chinese design. Lucia wondered about the weight and heat of the triple necklace of ornate silver balls that hung around Dorothy's neck. She started slightly as Dorothy Hoffman turned bold dark eyes on her and asked, "And what role do you play in this debacle, Miss Ramos?" The polite smile did not hide the venom in her voice.

"I am a homicide detective hired by Ms. Traeger as a consultant," Lucia responded.

"Indeed. Well, the whole affair is a ruinous scandal, in my opinion. Very likely to destroy Heritage House. Reputation is everything in this type of facility. I shall not stay despite all of Rex Fletcher's whining."

"Will Mr. Banks be leaving with you?" Lucia asked.

Dorothy Hoffman simply ignored the question. Her smile never waivered.

"Homosexuality and murder cannot be tolerated." She flared her nostrils. Lucia noticed that she did rather look like the actress who played Lou Grant's publisher. "No one of any breeding will want to move in. Then the apartments will be sold to a cruder type of person. After that, this shall not be a pleasant place at all. Not at all."

"Do you know of anyone who might have had a reason to kill Lorretta Millett?"

"Certainly not. You think I've done it, don't you?" Dorothy pointed a thin finger in Lucia's direction. "Well, it's ridiculous. Earl was about to pay off that dreadful loan she made him. Then she would have had no way to keep her claws in him. Why would I bother to kill her when I was about to win?" She seemed to tremble from the coldness of her anger. "If it was anyone, it was that depraved homosexual, that Margaret Traeger. She must have done it. After all, she had no moral sense whatsoever or she would not have yielded to such depravity. All of them are totally devoid of any respect for law and order." She gestured toward the kitchen. "Would you like a glass of iced tea or a cup of coffee? It would only take a moment."

Lucia shook her head, unsure what to ask next. "Earl Banks told you of his loan from Mrs. Millett?"

"Certainly. We are very close. I did so want him to be free of her, but, of course, lending him money was out of the question for me." Her smile never varied. Lucia was beginning to wonder if it was a plastic prosthesis that kept it in place.

"May I ask why?"

"Because Earl, despite his many sterling qualities, is a compulsive gambler. He hasn't a penny to his name. His wife tied everything up in a trust that pays his expenses. Frankly, Miss Ramos, none of this is any of your business. You know very well that Margaret Traeger is the murderer and it is insufferably rude for you to be asking these questions. I don't know why I ever agreed to speak to you. It must be the heat. I shall get more water pills from Dr. Fuller. You'll have to go now." She rose from her chair with her smile still in place. "Have a pleasant stay here in Mt. Vernon."

"Yes, thank you," Lucia said as the door closed.

Amy was back at the apartment by the time Lucia returned. "I dropped the books off at Ruby's. She seemed relieved to have a task and very happy with the bail hearing," she said.

"So what happened?"

She gave Lucia a complete description of the proceedings. "He didn't get her off on her own recognizance, but he did get bail reduced to one hundred fifty thousand dollars and he got the court to agree to accept a surety bond. I guess he's pretty good."

"He's earned his fee so far just by helping her avoid a bailbondsman," Lucia said, pouring herself a glass of water. "So when is she out?"

"They said all the paperwork would be done by five. We're supposed to pick her up then." Amy reached her arms around Lucia's waist and hugged her. "Have I told you lately that I love you?"

Lucia finished her drink, then turned around in Amy's arms. "Nope. Not in the last couple of hours anyway." She kissed Amy thoroughly. "Now, I guess we can either spend the rest of the afternoon making love or working the case. What's your pleasure, querida?"

"Pleasure is always my pleasure, but duty calls," Amy sighed. "So what's left to do—did you run into any leads?" She led Lucia into the living room.

"Some. Dorothy thinks Earl is a compulsive gambler who owed Lorretta money. I know he's an egomaniac. His living room is set up like a theater and he played the piano the whole time I was there. He gave me a rundown of Lorretta's long, sad life. She lost a father, a husband, and a son to various wars."

Amy shook her head. "And then disowned her only remaining child when he wouldn't go to Vietnam."

"Earl thinks 'only remaining son' is the killer, or perhaps the grandson. But he's definite on money being the motive."

"Just like her family."

"Yes. And Dorothy Hoffman is weird. She says these terribly mean things and smiles the whole time. It's really eerie. She didn't talk very long before she threw me out."

"What? A woman who's immune to your charms, Officer Ramos? I'm astonished!" Amy teased her.

"I really miss my badge. People have to talk to you when you're a cop. Ruth Hanckel wouldn't have, though. She only talked because she thought I was Native American like she is."

"Don't many Mexican-Americans have native blood?"

"Yeah. But that isn't the big news. Ruth cleaned this apartment on Saturday after Lorretta Millett died. And she emptied the trash cans. That means the empty bottle of digi-talis was put in the trash on Saturday afternoon or later."

"Aunt Meg was framed."

"It's beginning to look like that."

"How did they get in?"

"Same way they got into Lorretta's apartment. With a key. Everyone around this place has access to keys. Security stinks."

"But her family isn't likely to have access to Aunt Meg's key."

"Unless they found one in Lorretta's apartment."

"Labeled?"

"She seemed the methodical type."

"It could be. Seems to me we're developing a likely group of other suspects, just like the lawyer asked us to."

"Not enough to get the charges dropped," Lucia said.

"It would help if we knew when the digitalis was put in her sugar shaker."

"Amy, I know a lot about gunshot wounds and stabbing wounds. I have studied the effects of beatings. But I don't know a damn thing about poison. I think I'm going to need some help on this evidence."

"Well, we're sure not going to get it from Dr. Fuller. What about that friend of Freddie Christian's, the one that works at the hospital? It's worth a try."

Lucia agreed and called the hospital to set up an appointment. There was just enough time to drive to Mobile, talk for an hour, and get back to Citronelle to pick up Meg from the jail. Helen Frances seemed to be waiting for her call. She agreed to the time set.

"Well, that's great, but a little surprising that the director of a large hospital would be free on such short notice," Amy commented.

"Now that you mention it, she was a little reluctant. I bet she had to cancel something to work us in. Kind of strange. I guess she and Freddie Christian are very good friends. I'm glad we stayed on Freddie's good side. I think she would be a dangerous enemy," Lucia responded, gathering her case notes into a stack.

"Let me get something for Aunt Meg to wear home. All she has at the jail is her nightgown."

"Sounds good to me. I like seeing your aunt in her nightie. She's a great-looking woman." Lucia leered at Amy.

"You're a terrible lech, Ramos. No woman is safe around you." Amy kissed her cheek, then disappeared into the bedroom. She returned with a garment bag and an overnight case.

Lucia put all her case notes into her briefcase and they left. With keys scattered in many hands, they would never again trust the security of Heritage House apartments.

After putting Meg's clothes in the trunk, Lucia unlocked Amy's door and went around to the driver's side of the Skylark. Her heart stopped with Amy's scream. She rushed back to the other side of the car. Coiled on Amy's seat was a fairly large snake with mottled brown markings. It hissed loudly. Lucia jumped back from the open door and slammed it shut.

"That looks like a cottonmouth." She shuddered.

"Have you seen one before?" Amy asked timidly.

"No, but it sounds like what I've had described to me. I'm not getting close enough to check the shape of the tail. We need to call the sheriff. I think someone is trying to close down our investigation the quick and dirty way."

They ran back to Meg's apartment to call the sheriff's office. A confused woman kept telling them to call Animal

Control. "We don't arrest snakes," she finally said and hung up on them.

"I don't think she got it," Lucia said.

"What do we do now?" Amy asked furiously. She paced back and forth in the small dining room. "Wait to get shot?"

"That doesn't seem to be this murderer's style. Too straightforward. We'd better call Helen Frances and cancel that appointment." Ms. Frances graciously rescheduled for Friday morning. Lucia detected a note of relief in her voice. The original appointment had probably been at a bad time. Lucia was impressed anew at Freddie's influence. She turned her attention back to the snake. "I suppose we either call Animal Control or trap the snake ourselves."

"Are you insane, Lucia Ramos? That snake could kill you."

"Not likely. I watched my grandmother get snakes out of her kitchen when I was a kid. All we need is a trash can and a broom."

"Lucia, you are absolutely not to do this. I forbid it." Amy's voice got louder.

"Relax. The only time you need to worry about getting bitten is when you don't know the snake is there. I won't get any closer than the length of the broom. I'll be safe," Lucia said with more assurance than she felt.

"Why don't we just leave the door open and let it slither away like sensible people would?" Amy pleaded.

"Then the sheriff will never believe us. I think we'll be safer from attack if somebody believes us. And he won't believe it unless he sees the snake. So he'll have to see the snake and we'll have to catch it," Lucia said with finality.

"What if it wraps itself around the broom and crawls up it and bites you?"

"Well, I guess that will prove it was a murder attempt, won't it? Relax, Amy. I know what I'm doing. That snake isn't a malevolent demon. It's just a small, hot, scared animal."

"Small? It's as long as my arm." Amy spat the words out.

"It doesn't weigh as much as your cat. I know. I had a pet snake when I lived at mi abuela's."

"She let you keep a snake in the house?" Amy was stunned.

"Well, not in the house. It did come in a couple of times, but she just swept it out the door."

"Lucia, this snake is not a pet."

"No, but I can handle it. Where's the broom?"

Amy pointed wordlessly to the coat closet by the door.

"Great. And a trash can, a big one?"

"There's one in the trash room a couple of doors down. We can get it on our way out." She shook her head at her own foolishness as she guided Lucia to the immaculate trash room. They lifted the partially full plastic bag out of it. Then Lucia gave Amy the broom and picked up the battered metal container. Amy shouldered the broom like a rifle and saluted. "I hope you're not crazy, general, sir."

Lucia grinned. "I hope I'm not too." They carried their capture tools into the parking lot. "It may have died from the heat. I don't see it on the seat. It probably crawled under one of them to get cool."

"Great. How do we get it out?"

"Poke at it with the broom. It gets mad usually and comes out." Lucia opened the door and stepped back quickly. There was no sign of the snake.

"Maybe we just imagined it."

"Right. You want to slide onto that seat and find out?"

"No. I think I'll pass. Now, you just poke around with the broom and it comes out. Then what?"

"I flip it into the trash can."

"Right. This I want to see."

Lucia began to poke under the passenger seat. There was no response. "Let's try the other side." She closed the door and moved the trash can and broom to the driver's side. She repeated her poking. The snake came out of its hiding place obviously angry. Lucia slipped the broomstick under the snake and lifted it up. The broom hit the steering wheel and the snake was jarred off. It slithered out of the car. Amy screamed and ran back toward the apartments. Lucia quickly stepped back a couple of paces and tipped the trash can to its side. She flipped over the broom and used the wide end to sweep the snake into the container. Quickly she tipped it back up. The angry snake hissed at the bottom. She was drenched in sweat.

Amy walked back to the car. "I can't believe you did that. You are a very brave woman."

"Or a very foolish one," Lucia retorted. "Shall we take our prisoner to jail?"

"I would like to report an attempted murder," Lucia said to the clerk in a firm, official voice.

"Yes, ma'am. I'll have to get the sheriff for that. I only handle reports of misdemeanors. You know, like dog fights and such."

"Dog fights?" Amy whispered to Lucia.

"Like cock fights. It's illegal in most states," Lucia whispered back.

"I hear you got a complaint of attempted murder?" Sheriff Cook's face was a reflection of his sour mind. "Someone take a shot at you for trespass or something?"

"No. Someone put a poisonous snake, a cottonmouth, I believe, inside our rental car," Lucia replied evenly.

"I see. And it bit you and you almost died, right?" he asked.

"No. I was able to capture the snake without either of us being bitten. It happened approximately forty-five minutes ago in the visitors' parking lot of Heritage House." Lucia continued her report.

"Why didn't you call here instead of coming over if you thought someone was trying to murder you?" he questioned.

"Oh, they did, Sheriff Cook." The clerk broke in. "I told them to call Fred, since it seemed like an Animal Control problem."

"Uh huh." He paused a minute to think. "You got that there snake with you?"

"It's out in the car in a trash can," Lucia replied.

"Well, why don't you bring it in and we'll have a look at it." He reached in the pocket of his seersucker jacket and pulled out a cigar.

Amy turned away from the desk. "Let's get it, Lucia." She surreptitiously held her nose. Lucia followed her out into the humid sunlight. "He doesn't seem real excited about our report, does he?" she said.

"Not too excited, no. Here, I guess you get to hold the other side of this." They both peered down at the dark sinuous shape at the bottom of the battered metal trash can.

"I still can't believe you caught it," Amy said.

"I didn't think anyone would believe us if we didn't have the evidence. In case you haven't noticed, I don't think we're very well liked here." Lucia pushed open the swinging glass door.

"I noticed," Amy said.

"So bring it on over here, little ladies," the sheriff instructed, "and let me inspect your murder weapon. Louanne, you get me that yardstick out of the supply closet." He peered down at the snake as the clerk rose to get the ruler. "Never mind, Louanne, I don't need a poker with this here 'weapon.'" She sat back down. The sheriff started to laugh. "Ladies, your weapon here ain't loaded. Nope. This here snake ain't loaded." He shook with huge belly laughs. "This ain't no cottonmouth. It's got the wrong kind of head altogether." He grabbed either side of the trash can and jerked it up to flip the snake over. "Yep, it's an old yellow-belly, a fair-size one too. No poison at all."

"Why would anyone put that snake in my car? That's what I would like to know," Amy said.

"Now, Miz Traeger. Was your car door locked and all the windows rolled up tight?"

"It was locked, but I left the windows open a couple of inches to let the heat out."

Sheriff Cook nodded knowingly at the reply. "And I don't suppose you parked underneath any trees in the last couple of days, now, did you?" He puffed with satisfaction on his cigar.

"Yes, I suppose so. But what has that to do with someone trying to murder me with a poisonous snake?"

"Well, missy, the snakes round here on the Gulf coast get used to hanging around in trees, since they eat baby birds. Every now and then they just drop off a tree branch. I reckon one just landed on the roof of your little Japanese car and squirmed right in the window, thinking it was the best way to the ground. Kind of unusual, but it happens."

"About as often as alligators end up eating people in New York sewers, I'll bet. And it's an American car," Amy muttered under her breath.

"Now, Sheriff Cook, how come that snake didn't attack earlier? We haven't parked under a tree today, and we have spent a great deal of time in the car since yesterday morning, when we did park under a tree," Lucia probed.

"I got no idea. You'd have to ask the snake that. I'm no snake psychologist."

"That surprises me, Sheriff Cook. I would have thought you'd have a lot of insight into the mind of a snake." Amy muttered under her breath as she stomped out the door of the office.

"Well, thank you for your time, Sheriff," Lucia said.

"That's what I'm here for, little lady. Now don't you stand still under any trees, you might just meet up with another snake. They can be mean when they get messed with." He turned and went back toward his private office. At the door he turned around. "You don't mind me taking your evidence home, now, do you? My missus makes real fine snake stew, and I haven't had time to go snake hunting since I was elected sheriff."

"No problem, Sheriff Cook. You're welcome to it," Lucia said as she left.

"You'll never believe what the sheriff is going to do with our snake," she said, swinging into the passenger seat.

"What? Mount it as a trophy to stupidity?"

"Nope. Eat it."

"Ugh. Where to now? It's over an hour until Aunt Meg is released. What should we do?"

"I think the medical examiner has an office in Citronelle. We should drop by and see if he's free for a chat. Boy, do I miss my badge."

"Why now?" Amy asked pulling onto U.S. 45.

"No one has to be polite or even talk to me. The sheriff hates us. The informants throw me out halfway through the interview, and I haven't any idea how to make the ME co-operate. I feel like a failure and I'm so embarrassed about that snake I could die. I was so sure it was a cottonmouth. Now I'm not at all sure it was a murder attempt. Maybe someone just wanted to scare us."

Amy pulled up in front of a convenience store. "I hope it gives him indigestion. Do you want me to call Dr. Roberts? He's the ME, right? I'm sure that was the name on the autopsy report, Dr. Fritz Roberts."

"No, I'll call him," Lucia said, opening her door. She came around to Amy's window and rapped on it. "They could have given us a ticket for parking in a no-parking zone." Amy stuck her tongue out and waved Lucia toward the pay phone. In a few moments she was back. "He'll be free in fifteen minutes. His office is two blocks to the right."

In a couple of minutes they were parked in front of a

converted two-story house. The lawn was neatly trimmed with straight edges to separate it from the geraniums that bordered the walk. A workman perched on scaffolding was applying green paint to the roof trim. He waved his roller at Lucia and Amy as they passed. "Hot enough for ya?" he called down.

"I do believe it is," Lucia responded just before they entered the vestibule that had once been a front porch.

"We're here to see Dr. Roberts," Amy said to the young woman seated behind a green metal desk.

"Those women are here, Uncle Oz," she shouted into an ancient intercom.

"Thanks, I'm almost done," a male voice answered back.

"Have a seat. He'll be right with you," she said, then bent back over the papers on her desk. She carefully inserted three carbons and folded the thick pack of paper into an old Royal typewriter. The keys had to be struck hard.

Lucia watched the young woman carefully consider each letter as she struck it. Amy settled down with an archival copy of Family Circle magazine to read about "25 Christmas Presents to Make for Less Than 25 Dollars." After about ten minutes the door from the interior opened and a woman in her forties wheeled herself through it.

The receptionist nodded to the patient as she led them down the central hall of the house. "He's in his office behind the second door on the left."

A mural of hot air balloons on a light blue background covered all four office walls. A rotund man with white hair sat behind an immense peacock blue desk.

"Please, have a seat. I'm Oz Roberts, the medical examiner for Tensaw County. My appointment to the august office is due more to my lack of competition than to my expertise as a pathologist. I am the only resident doctor in the county. So, please make allowances. Now, how may I help you?"

"Dr. Roberts, we..." Amy began.

"Please, dear, call me Oz. I've been stuck with the name ever since someone noticed my resemblance to the wizard in the Judy Garland movie. In fact, I've grown rather fond of it since I consider much of the practice of medicine a snake-oil show." He pushed his office chair away from the desk and propped his feet up on an open drawer.

"We'd like to talk about the autopsy. The report in Sheriff Cook's file was a little sketchy," Lucia commented.

"Yes. Well, Dorothy, my niece, is not the world's best typist so I try to keep everything as brief as possible." A warm smile crossed his face at the mention of his niece/receptionist. "What did you need to know?"

"How did you proceed? Did you look at the heart first?" Lucia asked.

"Yes. It was very healthy. No sign of any deterioration at all. Very unusual for a woman her age. Arteries were as clean as a whistle. Her heart would have been remarkable in a thirty-year-old athlete, much less a seventy-year-old woman. The minute I saw it I knew why her daughter-in-law insisted on an autopsy. Besides, Mrs. Millett looked too peaceful. Heart attack is very painful; your face gets all distorted by pain."

"Did you find anything unusual?"

"Not that I know of." He opened his hands, palm up. "Look, I'm the last of a breed, an old-time country doctor. I'm great with sore throats and cuts. I can stitch up a gunshot wound, but I'm only a mediocre pathologist at best. The county commission appointed me because I'm close and I'm cheap. But the vast majority of the deaths in this county aren't a complex puzzle. Most are due to natural causes. The rest are usually obvious, a stab wound to the heart, a bullet in the head. It doesn't take much sophistication to testify competently to that kind of death. A death like Mrs. Millett's happens maybe once in a decade."

"Are you saying you didn't feel competent doing her autopsy?" Amy asked in surprise.

"Absolutely. If that tox report hadn't come back with the digitalis on it, I would have insisted that the body be shipped down to Mobile for a thorough review." He nodded his head as punctuation. "I may not be a magnificent pathologist like the one in Cornwell's mysteries, but there is one great talent I have: I know what I don't know."

Lucia rubbed her hand against her cheek and chin while she thought. "Okay, Dr. Oz, think about the report from the point of view of a nonprofessional. What might we miss because of what we don't know? Was there anything unusual that only a medical professional would notice?"

"Let me review it with that in mind." He whirled his chair around to pull a file from a rose-colored file case behind him. Dr. Oz spread the papers across his desk and examined them. "Degeneration in the olfactory nerve. She couldn't smell or taste much."

"I wondered about that. Does digitalis taste bad? Wouldn't she have noticed it in the cinnamon sugar?" Lucia asked.

"Probably not. It's not a very strong taste, kind of metallic. Silver comes to mind as a comparison. Now that you mention digitalis, I was a bit surprised when they arrested an elderly woman." He picked a sheet of paper up and examined it. "Yes, just as I remembered."

"What is it?" Amy prodded.

"This is the toxicology report on the fragments that hadn't been completely crushed into powder, found mixed in with the cinnamon sugar. The dosage of the pills found in the sugar shaker was twice what would normally be prescribed for the elderly." He tapped a yellow pen against his chin. "Quite unusual for a rest home."

"Did you mention this in your report?" Lucia asked, taking notes as quickly as her hand could move.

"No, it didn't occur to me until now. The heavier dosage isn't at all unusual except with the elderly. They don't tolerate the larger dosage well. I didn't think a thing about it until just now. I'll certainly add that to my comments. Let me review the rest of the report. I'd hate to miss any other significant facts."

Lucia and Amy examined the hot air balloons on the wall to break the tedium of doing nothing while Dr. Oz examined each page of the report carefully.

"Yes, her blood electrolytes were off as a result of the action of a diuretic."

"What does that mean?" Lucia asked.

"She had been taking diuretics. A lot of the elderly do that. It seems to increase their tolerance for the hot, humid climate here. Too bad. It made her death from the digitalis very fast. Without them she might have survived. But maybe not. I don't see anything else that might be useful. But thank you for adding a new tool to my study of pathology. The point of view of a layman is very helpful, very helpful indeed. I'm in your debt." He reached across the desk to shake their hands.

"I have one last question, Dr. Oz. It's personal so I won't take it as rudeness if you'd rather not answer, but why do you have balloons on your walls and all the bright colors in your office?"

"Not rude at all. I realize I'm going against the medical tradition of great dignity and sobriety. When I got the nickname, Oz, I spent a lot of time thinking about charlatans and magicians and wondering why people persisted in listening to them despite the constraints of logic. As I grew older, I began to realize that many of the conditions I dealt with were grievously affected by the mind and emotions of the sufferer." A wistful smile played around the corners of his mouth. "So many of the drugs prescribed to alleviate this suffering have side effects as bad as the disease. I have several patients who show Parkinson's symptoms from years of valium ingestion. It's very sad. So I decided that I would try a little prestidigitation of my own. I prescribe a scandalous amount of vitamins, I have a well-stocked supply of placebos, and I have balloons painted on my wall."

He looked at the puzzlement on his visitors' faces. "I see I still haven't clarified this. I try to give my patients hope, cheerfulness and courage, the cardinal virtues of good health, both mental and physical. The balloons, the bright colors are to signify cheerfulness. If you won't report me to the AMA, I'll admit I've prescribed painting them on the walls of a patient's home, a specific for postpartum depression, especially when mixed with a small party to celebrate the new mother's importance in the life of her baby."

"How wonderful!" Amy exclaimed.

"Thank you. Praise is important in maintaining the three cardinal virtues, so I accept your dose with delight." He walked around his desk and gave Amy a brief hug. Then his pudgy fingers pulled a white flower from behind her ear and he presented it to her. He did likewise for Lucia. "Now, fair ladies, I really must see my next patient. Adieu."

The smiles he had given them lasted all the way to the car. Lucia and Amy opened their doors and waited for the hottest air to escape. Rolling the windows all the way up had its cost.

"That doctor is a real magician," Lucia commented.

"Let's move to Citronelle. I'd love to have him for my physician. I wouldn't care a bit if I was sick. What an absolute delight of a man," Amy replied, sliding into the driver's seat.

"He does give one courage, doesn't he? And the information on the digitalis is great. Together with Ruth's testimony about emptying the wastebasket, that really weakens the link in the only physical evidence the DA's got. I felt like singing the 'Hallelujah Chorus.' " Lucia snapped her seatbelt into place and closed her door.

"Why not?" Amy asked as she switched on the air conditioner to maximum. She broke into an off-key version of the chorus and Lucia chimed in. They repeated it all the way to the courthouse. Lucia was still humming it at the entrance to the jail as she held the luggage in either hand.

"I'll wait out here. It's faster than them having to search all this," she said to Amy as the door slid open. Amy nodded and went inside alone.

About fifteen minutes later, she emerged with her arm around Meg, who was wearing a nightgown. Both their faces were covered with tears. They both put their free arms around Lucia and hugged her tightly.

"The matron said there was a bathroom on the first floor I could use to change and put my make-up on," Meg said rather desperately. Amy and Lucia waited outside while Meg fixed herself up. She looked like a new person with her hair swept up into a bun and a touch of color on her lips and cheeks. Amy breathed a sigh of relief to see her look like herself again.

"I'd like to call Ruby, but not from here," Meg said, allowing Lucia to take the empty garment bag from her arms.

"There's a pay phone not far from here that we've been using," Amy offered.

Meg almost ran from the car to the phone. Amy and Lucia watched her from the car.

"I gather you told her that we had dinner with Ruby and she told all," Lucia said, turning the fan down low on the air conditioner.

"More or less," Amy said. "Maybe I should turn the car off. I hate to waste gas."

"Too hot. It looks like she's hanging up. That was quick." Lucia reached behind to open Meg's door for her.

"Do you girls mind meeting Ruby for dinner here in Citronelle?" Meg asked.

"Fine with me," Lucia replied. "I didn't bother to eat lunch and I'm starved."

"Me too," Amy admitted, pausing at the entrance to the parking lot. "Which way?"

"Take a left instead of a right on Highway 96. There's a wonderful barbecue restaurant called Powdrell's run by a black family from New Mexico. Ruby knows their father."

The scent of cooking meat and hickory smoke permeated the neighborhood. The restaurant, like many of the businesses in Citronelle, was in a converted house. A large smokehouse had been built on to the back of the house with a covered and screened walkway joining them.

They were ushered into a small private room with only one table. A reserved sign was plucked from the table by the high-school-aged African-American youth who escorted them to the room.

After they were seated, Meg reached across the table to grasp their hands. "I can't thank you girls enough. I don't know what I would have done without you. All my years in law ill-prepared me to be a prisoner. I was so in a panic I couldn't think what to do." A shudder passed through her. "Being powerless and vulnerable made me regress to my unpleasant childhood. The people weren't terrible or abusive except that sheriff. The night matron in particular was very kind. But I was so frozen with fear I could not get my mind to work. I hope I never have to go back."

"Would you like to know what we've found out?" Amy asked.

"Please. I find it very reassuring that you were investigating on my behalf."

"The sheriff isn't looking for any other suspects, so it's a good thing we are. I just wish I didn't have to leave Sunday," Lucia commented.

"But we've put lots of holes in their case," Amy hurried to say.

"I guess I'm relieved, although it seems uncharitable," Meg said, smiling.

"Her son and her grandson both had strong motives, access to digitalis, and could easily have had the opportunity to put it in the sugar shaker," Lucia summarized.

"Do you think they did it?"

"Not really. The grandson is only twelve and he doesn't seem like a monster. I think he was fond of his grandmother in a distant sort of way." Lucia began tracing the edges of the red and white checks on the tablecloth while she talked. "Her son's hatred seemed pretty distant, too. When I try to imagine either of them as the murderer I keep wondering why now? Why not ten years from now or two years ago? Besides, I don't think they'd know enough about Heritage House gossip to try to frame you."

Meg leaned forward. "You think I was intentionally framed?"

"We think so, Aunt Meg. But we don't know by whom. Do you have your digitalis with you?"

"Of course. I don't move a step unless it's with me. Except in jail, of course, where the matron kept it." She withdrew a cloisonné pill box from the slash pocket in her grey linen slacks.

"I was hoping it would be in the prescription bottle. Do you know what dosage it is?" Lucia asked.

"Twelve point five or one twenty–five or something like that. I'm not sure where the decimal goes."

"Half the dosage of the medicine found in Lorretta Millett's sugar shaker," Amy announced triumphantly.

"I presume that's good news," Meg said.

"Very good news. Speaking of good stuff, what should I order?" Lucia asked.

"Everything's good, but Ruby and I'll split a plate of barbecued chicken in deference to our cholesterol. The slaw is nice, not that sort of milky glop you get in some restaurants," Meg suggested. "Now, what is so important about the dosage of my pills?"

"Means. You had the means to poison Lorretta with your

strength prescription only if she was killed with that level, but not with one at twice that level. The DA will have to prove that you had access to pills of the higher dosage. Maybe he can, but maybe he can't. And it makes the empty prescription bottle in your trash useless as evidence." Lucia paused to take a sip of beer.

"We think someone planted that bottle in your room because Ruth, the housecleaner, said she emptied your wastebasket about noon on Saturday," Amy said, drawing lines in the condensation on her large glass of lemonade.

"How are the ribs?" Lucia asked, peering at the menu.

"I've only had them once and they were quite good, but rather fatty."

Lucia sighed. "They always are. What are you having, Amy?"

"Beans, slaw, cornbread, and watermelon."

"That's no help. Maybe I'll have the barbecued beef sandwich."

"Good choice," Ruby said from the doorway of the private dining room. Meg threw herself into Ruby's arms. Ruby deftly kicked the door shut behind them. Despite being five inches shorter, Ruby managed to completely enfold Meg in a comforting hug. "Don't you ever scare me like that again, sweetness. My heart went cold when I saw them put those handcuffs on you. I couldn't stand it, not knowing how you were. You've got to release me from that ridiculous promise immediately, you wretch, or I will be forced to break it and you know that would wound my honor." Ruby was forced to quit talking as Meg kissed her passionately and deeply.

Amy flushed and tried not to watch, but she was fascinated by her aunt's obvious arousal. Lucia took Amy's hand and stroked it. "Perhaps we should go to the bathroom, mejita, and give these lovers some time alone." Ruby nodded her gratitude at the suggestion and moved away from the door so Lucia and Amy could slip out.

Fifteen minutes later Amy knocked lightly on the door to the small dining room. "Come in," Meg's voice responded.

"Thank the Goddess," Amy whispered to Lucia. "It was getting a little embarrassing, hanging around the bathroom that long."

Ruby and Meg were holding hands at the table in the security afforded by the private room. "Leave the door open," Ruby said. "Then they'll come for our dinner order. Meg said that you have evidence that may get the charges dropped. That's wonderful."

"I'm not sure it will get the charges dropped, but it does call into question the only physical evidence they've got," Lucia amended as she sat back down in her chair.

"So who goes first? You with your news or me with mine?" Ruby asked.

"What news?" Amy answered. "Did you find out something from those books of Lorretta's?"

"Not much, but what I did find was very interesting. That book on the Olympics, for example. I must have stared at every page for ten or fifteen minutes until I got it." She took a copy of a photograph out of her leather notebook and handed it to Meg. "Recognize anyone?" she asked.

Meg cocked her head as she carefully examined each face in the team lineup. "That one," she said, pointing to a figure, "could be Henry Hoskins' son. It looks so much like him."

"Bingo, my dear. Except it isn't his son, it's Henry himself. Or Heinrick Hoehn, as he is labeled in this picture." She passed the photograph to Lucia.

"That's right," Meg said, "He said something at dinner one night about winning a medal in the Olympics. Lorretta must have looked it up. He looks very dashing."

"Quite handsome," Lucia said passing the photo to Amy. "But why did he change his name?"

"A lot of people with German names did that during World War II," Meg commented.

"But he had more reason than most," Ruby said. "Look carefully at the insignias on his collar. They're hard to see in that picture, so I enlarged it a couple of times. It makes his face hard to recognize, but it really clarified the lightning slashes. He wasn't on the American team. He was on the German team."

"SS," Meg said, shocked.

"A Nazi? This man was a Nazi?" Amy asked.

"Distilled Nazi. More Nazi than most. He was in the branch of Nazis reserved for the most faithful and the most vicious," Ruby answered triumphantly.

"And he lives right across the hall from Lorretta. She must have known if she had this picture," Meg added.

"She probably confronted him with it, like she did you about your lesbianism," Amy said. "And maybe he killed her to keep her quiet."

"Maybe," Lucia said. "But we're walking down the same road the sheriff took. Assuming someone is a murderer because they belong to a group you despise. We should at least talk to him before we jump to any conclusions."

Ruby and Meg looked at each other. "I'm not sure how helpful that would be," Meg said. "Henry is getting a little vague."

"Henry is a lot vague. We think he has Alzheimer's and his wife Willa is covering for him. If he gets diagnosed with the Big A, he gets locked up on the Alzheimer's ward and they can't live together anymore," Ruby cut in. "My money is on Willa as murderer rather than Henry. She'd do anything to protect him."

At that moment their dinner arrived and everyone set to eating with enthusiasm. Amy spread butter over the hot cornbread and watched it melt immediately into the rough yellow surface. Ruby and Meg set the chicken plate between them and shared with the ease of long familiarity. Lucia's beef sandwich dripped sauce as she took a big bite. For a few minutes, the only sounds were those signifying deep enjoyment of the dinner. The young man pulled the door closed behind himself.

"No wonder Henry and Willa were so careful around Lorretta," Meg said during a pause in her eating.

Ruby swallowed a bite of cornbread, then commented, "You noticed that too."

"But neither of these secrets seems important enough to kill someone over," Meg said, picking up her half of the dill pickle. "They're embarrassing but..."

"Blackmailers are sometimes killed to prevent embarrassment," Lucia said, then returned her attention to the sweet tangy sauce she was dipping her sandwich in. Amy touched her chin to signal Lucia that a drop of sauce had landed there. Then it struck her that discretion was unnecessary. She reached over and wiped it off with her fingertip. Lucia caught Amy's finger between her lips and nibbled on it.

Meg smiled indulgently. Ruby covered her hand and caressed it. "By the way," she said, "Maggie and I have changed our plans. We'll be staying here in Citronelle in a motel until this is settled. I went by her apartment and picked up some things. We don't want to hang around Heritage House and endure the gossip."

Meg nodded her agreement. "I hate to be a poor hostess, but I'm not ready to deal with the public yet. This seems more private."

"We'll treat it like a second honeymoon," Ruby said, lifting one eyebrow.

"Fourth or fifth by now," Meg corrected.

"I'm curious, Meg. I was a little startled when Ruby called you Maggie. Then the people I talked to today referred to you as Margaret. Which do you prefer?" Lucia asked.

"Frankly, Margaret seems appropriate for people I only consider acquaintances. But Meg is just fine, Lucia." Meg suddenly turned her attention to the bowl of beans between her place setting and Ruby's.

"Maggie, I think the girls deserve a little more honesty," Ruby said. "It's more important than not hurting someone's feelings. They look pretty tough to me."

"Ruby, I could kill you," Meg said, half-vexed.

"Don't say that around the sheriff, love."

Amy broke in. "Please do be honest. I promise not to be shattered."

"It's only...well..." She stared at her plate. "Meg is what your father called me. Because of that I have never favored the name."

"Oh, shit," Amy said. "I'm sorry. I knew he called you Meg, but I had no idea it hurt you so. I should have listened to Ruby. She tried to tell me." She lost all interest in her meal. She didn't even notice that her left hand was still holding a spoonful of beans.

"Of course you didn't, Amy," her aunt said. "How could you have possibly known? Besides 'Aunt Meg' was your name for me. I didn't mind..."

"Margaret Traeger," Ruby said in a warning voice.

"...very much," Meg continued weakly. A bite-size piece of chicken at the end of her fork seemed to fascinate her. She didn't lift her eyes off it during the entire discussion of her name.

"I think I'd like to call you Maggie," Lucia offered.

"I'd like that, Lucia," she replied, keeping her eyes downcast.

"I would too," Amy said. "And I'd like to drop the aunt. I think it's time you became my friend instead of my surrogate mother. That is, if you would be comfortable with it."

Maggie raised her eyes as a beatific smile spread across her face. "I'd like that very much." The fork with the chicken dropped to her plate, then Maggie reached over to take Amy's hand.

"See, Traeger, I told you no one would die," Ruby laughed.

"Nope, no one is even upset," Amy said clasping her aunt's hand.

The conversation returned to the investigation as everyone ate their fill. Lucia summarized her interviews and Maggie told her about the arraignment. When everyone was satisfied that they had exhausted every nuance of the day, Ruby reopened the door so they could get the bill. Ruby handed the waiter several twenties before he could put it on the table. "My treat, girls. A reward for a job well done." A chorus of thank yous followed her gesture.

"Would you mind putting Ruby's beads on her door tonight?" Maggie asked. "I'd rather people not notice she's away tonight."

"Sure," Amy said.

"I'm going to be involved in this one way or the other, Maggie," Ruby warned.

"I'd like to get home and make some appointments with the rest of the bridge club," Lucia said as she dropped her napkin next to her plate. "And the Hoskinses, if they'll talk to me."

"Aren't we done?" Amy asked. "Surely, with the pill dosage not matching Maggie's prescription, the charges will be dropped, won't they?" She pushed her chair back from the table but didn't get up.

Lucia shook her head. "Afraid not. They might be, but more likely they won't be. The DA doesn't have a great case but if he drops it now, well..."

"He might look like the horse's ass that he is." Ruby finished Lucia's sentence for her.

"Yeah." Lucia pushed her chair back and stood. "And that won't help him get reelected. If he keeps the case going and loses, he can always blame it on the jury."

"Shit, shit, and double shit," Amy cursed.

"Shit," Maggie said, to everyone's surprise. "Well, if I'm going back to jail, I'd better make good use of my limited freedom." She stood. "Come on, Ruby, let's go to bed." Ruby followed her out of the tiny dining room, leaving Amy and Lucia to dissolve in laughter.

Amy pulled into the visitors' spot nearest the back door of Heritage House and both women rolled their windows up tight. "One snake a week is about my quota," Lucia quipped as she gathered all her notebooks out of the back seat.

"Or perhaps a decade," Amy responded, checking the car doors to be sure they were locked. She took Maggie's luggage out of the trunk. "I wish we had some way of securing the door to the apartment. I'd hate to wake up with a knife at my throat."

"Not this murderer's style. But we should check the apartment for scorpions and so on. You know, Amy, I just can't quite picture any of these old ladies tossing a snake in our car. I don't believe for a minute that it dropped out of a tree. Maybe we're dealing with two people. Maybe Mrs. Hoskins poisoned the sugar and Mr. Hoskins put the snake in our car. I wonder if the person who put the snake in our car knew it wasn't poisonous. Maybe they were trying to scare us?" She noticed that they were at the door to Maggie's apartment. "Before we go in, could you show me where the washer is?"

"Next to the trash room. We passed it on the way to get the trash can. Oh no, Lucia, we left the trash can at the sheriff's office. I forgot all about it." Amy unlocked the apartment door, switched on the light, and looked around carefully before she went in.

"Petty larceny. Amy, you're leading me into a life of crime." Lucia began to give the living room a thorough inspection. When it appeared free of risk, she went on to the bedroom and bath. Amy went into the kitchen and, after carefully checking the cabinets and under the refrigerator, she put a pot of water on the small stove for tea.

"What are you making?" Lucia asked from the doorway.

"Pot of tea."

"Frankly, I think it would be safer to stick with tap water until we figure out who the murderer is. Putting digitalis in cinnamon sugar is pretty subtle. We'd better eat and drink at a cafe. It'll be safer. We'll pick up a few things for breakfast later."

"Good idea." Amy turned off the heat. "I think I'll take a shower. I can't imagine how they could booby-trap that."

"Too bad it isn't big enough for two. But I need to do laundry, put beads on Ruby's door, and call those other people for an interview." She went to the bedroom to gather her clothes. Amy followed. "Let's check under the covers just in case." She flipped back the blanket on her bed. Nothing slithered out. Amy checked her bed with the same results. She began to giggle.

"I feel like I've wandered onto the set of an Indiana Jones movie."

"Es la verdad," Lucia commented, stuffing her clothes into the pillowcase she had stripped off the pillow. "I'll be back in a second. Don't fall through a secret panel in the wall while I'm gone."

"Okey dokey. Lock the door behind you, okay?"

"Sure."

Lucia had to knock on her return, having forgotten to take a key. Amy, wrapped in a towel, opened the door.

"I already have all the magazine subscriptions I want, young lady," she said, laughing.

"But I'm selling magazines you need, lady. How about Yellow Silk, Deneuve, or Girl Jock, all at special subscription prices?" Lucia imitated the aggressive manner of a door-to-door salesperson. "Just let me in and I'll show you my special deals." She stuck her foot in the door.

"I'm more a Common Lives, Trivia, Lesbian Ethics sort of girl."

Their game was interrupted by a gruff-faced elderly man

striding past their door. He glared at them in disapproval. Lucia chortled as she stepped inside the door. "I hope that wasn't Mr. Hoskins. He didn't look real impressed."

"I doubt it. He looked much too alert to be suffering from Alzheimer's." Amy closed the door and shifted the towel from her body to her dripping hair.

"I'd better start my calls to set up tomorrow's appointments before it gets any later. I imagine some of the residents go to bed pretty early." Lucia began her phone calls. They went quickly and graciously. Lucia finished her laundry, pulling out the rattlesnake T-shirt to wear for a nightshirt.

"You're not going to wear that to bed after what happened today," Amy exclaimed.

Lucia settled in the recliner with a glass of tap water and her copy of Almanac of the Dead. "Sure. I figure it'll scare away any other snakes. I learned that from my grandmother. She hung those black clay tarantulas with metal legs around the house to keep them out. It must have worked. We never had tarantulas in the house unless my brothers brought them in for a tarantula race."

"A tarantula race?" Amy said weakly. She stood behind the recliner and caressed Lucia's shiny black hair.

"Yeah. They would tie black thread around the spiders and poke them with a stick to make them hop. Frankly, it was kind of a slow race because the tarantulas would jump higher rather than farther. Sometimes the one that just crawled across the floor would win." Lucia walked her fingers across her thigh like a spider. "But Abuelita would always make them take the spiders outside and let them go. She had a very tender heart even for spiders. I still miss her."

"You've lost three people you love to death, Lucia. I can't even imagine it. Your mother to TB, your grandmother, then Yolanda. It's so final. You can't just drop in for a visit or give them a call. They're gone. Do you wonder sometimes if that's why you became a homicide detective?"

"No. It's just a job, Amy. We needed the money. Yolanda got a work-study job in the biology lab, and I got a job with campus police as a security aide. When they offered me full-time, I couldn't afford to turn it down. There weren't that many jobs in Austin for a Chicana with a brand-new BA in sociology. Yolanda was still working on her Master's, but her scholarship was good through the PhD."

"I didn't realize you were putting her through her education." There was a none-too-subtle note of disapproval in Amy's voice.

"She was my esposa. Her scholarship only covered tuition. Of course I helped her. Then, when she completed her doctorate, she would get a good job and I would finish my Master's."

"After you followed her to her new job," Amy declared.

"Sure. Why not?" Lucia sounded puzzled at Amy's irritation.

"Well, it sounds pretty codependent to me. Like you were a good little wife. Did you do the dishes too?"

"Hey, what's wrong with you, Amy? I loved Yolanda and she loved me. We were family. It wasn't like we were going to win the Florida lottery or anything. We had to help each other, or neither of us was going to finish the degree she wanted. Yolanda wanted to teach in a university. She had to have a PhD. Social workers only need a Master's. If I hadn't taken the police job, we would have finished about the same time."

"But you never did get a Master's."

"Is that what's bugging you? That I didn't get an advanced degree? Are you ashamed of hanging around with me because no one calls me doctor?"

"No! It's not that at all, Lucia. It's just...well...I think you were taken advantage of, and that makes me angry."

"You have no right to that anger, Amy. How can you

judge someone you never met, someone I loved with every breath in my body?" Lucia ignored the tears streaming down her cheeks and kept her voice steady. "We were not some case study out of your journals to be dissected by psychologists. We were two people who loved each other and made decisions that were the best we knew how. You have no right to judge us, Amy. No right at all. Go read up on love. Is that in any of your textbooks? It sure wasn't in the sociology texts. Love. Not sickness, not codependency, not exploitation, just love. You don't even know what it means."

"Lucia, I'm sorry." Amy slid to her knees and rested her head in Lucia's lap. "I do know about love and it isn't knowledge that came from any textbook. I know it from Maggie and Laura and you. I was insufferably arrogant. I had no right to make any judgment of Yolanda. I never met her. But I wish I could. To thank her for what you had together. Sometimes, I...well, I get jealous of what you shared. I want it to be less than it was."

Lucia molded her hands to Amy's head. "It is a leaf in the flame, querida."

"A leaf?"

"A matter not only forgiven but gone, leaving no trace." She drew Amy from the floor onto her lap, enfolded her in two strong arms, and rocked her. "Your soul needs some rest, like your body and mind. Rest here, mejita. Rest here."

THURSDAY

Tap water cascaded over the can of frozen orange juice while Lucia retrieved the dark brown toast from the toaster. Amy poured boiling water into a short, squat silver teapot with a silver strainer dangling from its spout. She hummed "I'm a little teapot" while she poured.

Lucia turned from the toast to kiss Amy on the ear. "You're awfully cute, you know."

"Thanks. Compliments are a great way to start the day. Cream and sugar in your tea?" Amy responded.

"Not unless we bought them last night," Lucia said, buttering her toast.

"Right. We didn't, so it's black tea and toast." She carried the teapot and two mugs to the table and Lucia followed with a plate of toast, knives, and jam.

"Those interviews I did yesterday weren't very informative. Parts of them seemed rehearsed," Lucia suggested, munching her toast.

"You're right, but I don't want to upset people, especially Minerva Worthington. She's a friend of...uh...Maggie's. I don't want to do anything that might damage any of her support here." Amy spread apricot jam from the tiny new jar they had picked up with the bread, a stick of butter, and tea from a convenience store the night before. "No argument." Lucia replied. "She's going to need all her friends before this is over. But I'd like to get pretty tough with the Hoskinses. I didn't tell her about the picture from the Olympics. I'd like to spring it on them first thing and see how they react." Amy nodded her agreement, since her mouth was too full to talk. "I'm going to take all my notes with me. I don't want to leave anything lying around for someone to look at while we're out." Lucia brushed crumbs from her teal blouse.

The door to the Hoskins' apartment was opened by a stern-faced woman in her seventies. Her prim white dress was unrelieved by any accents. She wore no jewelry except for a wide, gold wedding band on her age-spotted left hand. She gestured them inside without a greeting.

"Yes," she said. "You're Margaret Traeger's niece and her friend. What do you want?"

Lucia laid her briefcase on the brown Formica top of the dining room table and opened it. She rummaged around for the piece of paper Ruby had given her the night before. Then Lucia handed Willa the copy of page twenty-seven from Striving. "Would you like to tell us about this?"

Willa wadded the paper into a tight ball and threw it to the floor. Then she stamped on it several times as if to kill it. "Henry is so proud of his Olympic skating, his mind keeps going back to it. And it twists around to ruin us, the one thing he is so proud of.

"It's too late, isn't it, to claim it isn't him? Over fifty years of hiding, all for nothing because of one picture he should have been able to show with pride." She ground the paper under the sole of her brown orthopedic shoes.

"The uniform . . ." Lucia suggested.

"SS. He was a clerk. He ordered uniforms, supervised laundrymen."

"In the death camps?" Amy asked.

"No!" Willa shrieked. "In Berlin. He knew nothing of death camps. He was an athlete. It was a make-work job to keep him an amateur. You know what I mean. It was all so he could skate. He was very good."

"A silver medal," Lucia prompted.

"Yes, and probably a gold in the 1940 Olympics if they hadn't been cancelled. He was an athlete, not a war criminal."

"Then why the secrecy?" Lucia asked.

"It was crazy. Everyone wanted revenge. I was a nurse there, in Berlin in 1945. People would swear to anything out of hatred. But Henry had done nothing evil. I believed him then, and I still do. He was just a magnificent athlete trying to find a way to skate. That's all."

"But that was a long time ago in another country...." Lucia let her voice trail off.

"There are those who never forgive, never forget, the Nazi hunters. We could never risk it. What would it do to our children? My son is the chief of police in Sweetwater, Illinois. He's thirty-eight. His life would be ruined. Who'd hire someone whose father was in the SS? My daughter married a Jewish man whose parents were killed in the camps. He'd hate her, divorce her. If it comes out that my husband had an SS job, our family is destroyed. Please, is there any way I can convince you . . ."

"You could talk to us about Lorretta Millett," Amy said. "We don't want anyone hurt the way my aunt was hurt. I see no reason for us to spread any rumors about your family."

Lucia gave Amy a look. If Maggie Traeger needed more suspects to get her off the hook, they couldn't afford to protect the Hoskinses. She took her notebook and pen out of the briefcase.

Willa nodded. She led them into the spartan living room. There were three unpadded ladder-back chairs and a leather-upholstered armchair. She motioned Lucia and Amy toward two of the ladder-backs and took the third one herself. An upholstered sewing bag hung by a wooden frame next to her chair. Willa took out a tiny green sweater and began to work on it with very small knitting needles. In a band across the chest was a design of golden yellow stars of David.

"Your husband isn't here," Lucia stated.

"No. He's out on the golf course. I didn't want him upset. He's . . . not well." Willa Hoskins' face was completely devoid of emotion.

"Someone mentioned that Lorretta and Earl Banks had a fight the evening before she died. Did you see or hear anything?" Amy asked.

"Everything. Our door was open and Earl was giving quite a performance right there in the hallway. It was just after dinner. I suppose he hoped she would give in out of embarrassment. He should have known better." She calmly looped the yarn over her needle.

"Why do you say that?" Amy prodded as Lucia took notes.

"She was a very determined woman. She had high standards and expected the same from everyone else. Embarrassment meant nothing to her when it came to what she considered a moral issue." Willa picked up the next stitch.

"What was the argument about?" Lucia said, looking up from her notes.

"Money. Earl was demanding more time to pay back a loan. Lorretta was immovable. She held a loan on his piano. If he didn't pay, she said she would sell the piano to cover the loan. She was very firm."

"And he was..." Amy left the phrase open.

"Very angry. He pounded on her door for quite some time."

"Do you think he was angry enough to kill her?" Lucia asked.

"Over a piano?" Willa shrugged without dropping a stitch. "Who knows?"

"Can you think of anyone else who might have had reason to murder her?" Lucia paused in her notetaking to look Willa in the eye.

"Besides me, my husband, Margaret Traeger, Earl

Banks, and Dorothy Hoffman? No, but Lorretta loved ferreting out secrets. There may have been dozens of others. I expect there were." She continued to knit.

"How did she tell you that she knew about your husband's past?" Amy asked.

"She invited us over for tea, which was unusual. Normally, we didn't socialize except at dinner. That book, Striving, was open to Henry's picture. She told me that the Nazis had killed her husband, but she wanted to be fair-minded. She tried to talk to Henry about his war experiences, but he would only talk about skating." She paused in her knitting. "He's never hurt anyone in his life. In some ways, he is a very simple man, proud of his family and his skating. I'm not sure he even believed that atrocities happened during the war. He doesn't dwell on unpleasant thoughts."

"And Lorretta?" Lucia prompted.

"She said she would continue to investigate. If she found my husband was more than a clerk, if he had harmed anyone, she would turn the files over to the authorities. She was always as good as her word. I don't believe she would have told anyone without talking to us first, even if she found something, which, of course, she couldn't."

Lucia thought a moment, then asked, "Do you know of anyone beside Earl Banks she loaned money to?"

"No. She didn't confide any of her personal financial affairs." The knitting continued as Willa cast off the row she had been working on.

"You were a nurse in Germany?" Lucia asked.

"Yes."

"When did you quit nursing?"

"I'm still licensed. I work a four-hour shift in the medical unit on Saturday catching them up on paperwork. It's not demanding," Willa replied.

"You work here in Heritage House?" Amy asked, the surprise obvious in her voice.

"Why not? The pay isn't much, but it occupies my time and, frankly, we can use the money. It hasn't been easy with all the constant increases in the fees." She nodded, agreeing with her own statement.

"Did you exchange keys with Lorretta Millett?" Lucia asked.

"Yes, it was convenient. My Henry is sometimes forgetful."

"I can't think of anything else. What about you, Amy?" Lucia stopped writing and turned slightly in her chair.

"No, I don't have any other questions. Thank you for being so helpful. And that sweater you're working on is lovely."

"It's for my first great-grandchild, due in two months." Pride radiated from her face. She pushed her needles into the sweater and rose to her feet. "My daughter's daughter is the mother. We're going to fly to Seattle to see the baby. I can't wait." The animation that Willa had been lacking early in the interview was now present. She followed Lucia and Amy to the door. "Thank you for keeping our secret. I promise you won't regret it."

Amy smiled and said, "I'm a therapist. I have a lot of practice keeping secrets. Thank you for your frankness. Goodbye."

Lucia also said goodbye, pulling the door closed behind them. "Why on earth did you promise we would keep that secret, Amy? Your aunt needs all the suspects we can find."

"Do you think she did it?"

"She had motive, means, and opportunity. I'm not sure I care if she's guilty. She probably even had access to the larger dosage of digitalis. She's a great suspect!" Lucia strode down the hall, her pace matching the vehemence of her tone.

"I don't think she's guilty." Amy kept pace with Lucia.

"He was in the SS. He was a Nazi."

"She wasn't."

"I'll never understand you. I thought you were desperate to get Maggie off."

"I am. And you'll notice I didn't promise complete confidentiality. I simply said I wouldn't spread rumors, and I won't. I don't intend telling anyone unless it's the only possible way to get the charges dropped."

They turned the corner into Maggie's wing and almost ran into a very elderly woman on a motorized wheelchair. She beeped a bike horn at them and grinned.

"Don't turn me in. I know I was exceeding the speed limit, but it's no fun poking along." She put her finger over her lips and winked as she pulled away from them.

"Hot rodder," Amy whispered with a chortle.

"Cute," Lucia replied. "I wonder if she's single?"

"You're not, Ramos." Amy keyed her aunt's door. "Can I get you a glass of tap water while you do the snake search?"

"Just rinse the glasses before you put anything in them. I've no idea what someone might do next to scare us off," Lucia said, heading for the living room. Her search was more perfunctory than the night before.

Amy was reading through Maggie's notes about Lorretta when Lucia finally sat at the table for her water.

"Listen to this, Lucia. 'Lorretta always wanted to talk about financial matters. She was very interested in the bank failures. At one bridge club meeting, she refused to let anyone at her table talk about anything except Neil Bush's involvement in the failure of his savings and loan. She seemed to have much more information on it than the TV or newspapers.' The consistent pattern in this woman's life is her fascination with money. Maybe we should look more carefully at her family than the bridge club?"

"I don't think we should cancel our next appointment."

"Of course not. I just meant that we should find out where the Milletts live and have someone look into their finances. We pretty much took them at face value. I wish we knew more about them."

Lucia closed her eyes and shook her head hard once. "We just took Willa Hoskins at face value. And how about Earl Banks? His finances sound messy to me."

"Yes, but how do we do this? I haven't any idea how to go about this kind of investigation."

"Me either. Maybe we should hire a private investigator. I bet Byrd knows one. Let's call his office."

Amy offered her the phone and listened while Lucia elicited the name of a private investigator. Then Lucia gave a complete summary of yesterday's conversations and the incident with the snake. She hung up.

"They'd like us to send them a more comprehensive report. No hurry. It'll be months before this comes to trial." Lucia took in a deep breath and slowly exhaled. "We're really not in this alone. Byrd's office has already hired an investigator in LA to look into the Milletts. They live in Long Beach and he has an office in Westminister. That part's taken care of. God, I can't tell you what a relief it is to know we have back-up."

"You don't like being a loner," Amy said with a smile.

"No mejita, I don't. Not by choice, at any rate. I grew up with lots of family and friends around. I'm used to it. I count on it. It's been hard to be here, so far from all that. I never realized until now how much I count on it." She reached over and took Amy's hand.

"And I never realized quite how much I counted on Aunt ...on Maggie until this happened. I can't let them put her in prison." A note of panic crept into Amy's voice.

"They won't, mejita. I think we have enough to convince a jury that there were a lot of people as likely to have murdered Lorretta Millett as your aunt."

"But you don't really think any of the people we've talked to did it, do you?" Amy asked.

"Frankly, I'm not convinced. Maybe yes, but more likely no. Who knows? Maybe it'll be this Minerva Worthington." She looked at her watch. "We might as well go over to her apartment. We'll be a little early, but not much."

"It's apartment A210, right?"

"Yeah, near Ruby's," Lucia replied. "I wonder how those two are doing? Your aunt seems to be in love." They picked up all the scraps of paper off the table and put them in Lucia's briefcase before leaving.

"It's very sweet," Amy said, pulling the door closed behind her. She checked the knob to be sure it was locked. "We should call them and have lunch."

"They should be up by now. It's almost eleven. Of course, they might be busy," Lucia leered at Amy. "We could go back inside and be busy too."

Amy gently whacked her on the arm. "No time, querida, no time. Maybe later." Their conversation lapsed.

Minerva ushered them into an apartment with spartan furniture but lush fabrics.

"Have you been to Guatemala?" Amy asked.

"A couple of years with the Peace Corps, back in the seventies," Minerva replied.

"The fabrics are lovely, Ms. Worthington," Lucia commented.

"Thank you, but please, call me Min. I feel that any friends of Meg's are already friends of mine. Would you like to see my pretties before we talk?"

"Surely," Amy replied.

"Not all of them are Guatemalan, as you can probably tell." She gestured toward a hanging towel rack that displayed what appeared to be elaborately embroidered towels yellow with age. "These belonged to my friend. Her mother brought them from the Ukraine. They are rushnyky. They're ceremonial; sometimes they were used almost like money. This next pattern is a stylized Tree of Life. Next to it is the traditional Mexican Tree of Life. And just beyond, an African rendering of petroglyph trees from magnificent weavers in Lesotho at the Helang Basali cooperative. And the sampler with a crude tree in the center is my own effort at age seven. I keep it there to remind myself what incredible effort as well as talent is involved in creating fabric art."

"This one is very different. I like it." Lucia pointed to a foot-square piece of decorated fabric.

"It's called 'Goddess Descendant,' a modern piece by Julia Wolfe. She uses xerography to reproduce pictures, in this case, Venus of Willendorf with the wings from Winged Victory. Then she makes the fabric shrink with embroidery and beading. I love that gold tinsel around the bottom. It's so outrageous. I found that in a fabric gallery in San Antonio. I was really looking for Mexican weavings, but this piece stole my heart."

"I'll have to look for her work. That's where we're from," Amy said.

"Lovely city. Cammy and I went there often. It was as close to foreign travel as we could get on a weekend. It certainly has grown in the last twenty years," Min said, leading them back to the small dining room table near the entrance.

"You will have lunch, won't you? I presumed from the time of the appointment that lunch was included." There was a hint of a plea in her voice.

Outmaneuvered, Amy and Lucia acceded to the meal.

Lucia pulled out a captain's chair from the oak dining room table and sat on the colorful thin pillows tied to back and seat. It was very comfortable. "Not all the growth in San Antonio is welcome. There's a lot more crime than when I was a teenager."

"Everywhere. That's one of the reasons we left Birmingham. An elderly neighbor of ours was mugged on his front lawn. It scared everybody, especially those of us who are getting a bit frail." Min shook her head. "I swore when I got old I wouldn't be nostalgic for the good old days, but ..."

"And now to have a murder strike in your refuge," Amy prompted.

Min continued the conversation while serving a beautiful shrimp in tomato aspic surrounded by endive. "And many of us don't have the option of moving anymore. We've put all of our life savings into the purchase of an apartment here. Your investment is refundable lesst hree percent a month, so once you've been here three years, it's not refundable. Just gone. And they keep raising the monthly service fee. Why, it was only $600 when Cammy and I moved in, over four years ago. Now it's up to $1,700 a month. If Cammy hadn't had a $100,000 life insurance policy, I would be penniless. I couldn't afford to stay, and I'd lose all my money when I left. I just don't know if we would have chosen old HH if they had told us they were going to triple the rent in three or four years." She poured a light pink liquid in the three iced tumblers. Lucia and Amy both tasted.

"Tamarind!" Lucia exclaimed.

"Quite delightful," Amy said. "Like lemonade only with a fuller flavor."

"I drank it a great deal in Guatemala. I've found nothing better to grant relief from heat and humidity. Not even those water pills Dr. Fuller recommends." She rested her glass back on its dark wood coaster.

"Isn't there anything in your purchase contract that prohibits these huge increases?"

"Well, not really. We've read them over thoroughly, and, as you know, Amy, your aunt is a lawyer. The contract says that the expenses will be prorated to each resident as a monthly service fee. That little weasel in sales, Rex Fletcher, actually told Cammy and I that it would go down as occupancy was at a higher rate."

"If it's prorated, that would make sense for it to go down," Lucia commented before taking another bite of the satin-smooth aspic.

Amy finished the bite she had piled at the end of a crisp white endive leaf and said, "But Maggie hasn't said a word of this to either of us."

"She doesn't want to worry you. Ruby has plenty of money and she has been paying part of your aunt's fee. I overheard that eavesdropping, so don't you let on that you know." Min savored a tiny shrimp before swallowing it.

"I don't understand why the expenses would triple like that," Lucia said.

"Let's let Min enjoy her lunch. She has hardly had time to put a bite in her mouth," Amy chided.

"It's fine. I take forever to eat these days anyway. I just don't have the voracious appetite I had as a girl. Besides, it's a real treat to have new conversation partners. We get so used to each other here we could script the conversation before it happens. No, I don't mind a bit.

"The expenses went way up when the medical center opened. I don't know why. It doesn't seem to me that anybody stays there for long. They either die or get better. But we are paying over $100,000 to Dr. Fuller now that the medical center is open."

"It wasn't open when you moved in?" Lucia quizzed.

"Sort of. There was a lovely nurse there. Well, actually she was a physician's assistant. Mrs. Dexter. She wrote prescriptions and supervised the other nurses and the aides. Anyone with anything serious was sent to Mobile and came back here to convalesce."

Amy blotted her lips with a heavy linen napkin, then folded it so the colorful birds were displayed above the raveled hem. "And now they handle the serious illnesses here?" she asked.

"No, not really. It seems to me we are getting pretty much the same care, but now it's costing four times as much. It has something to do with what you have to do to be a licensed medical facility to qualify for Medicare. Loretta was researching it for us."

"What?" Lucia asked, dropping her fork on her plate. "She was what?"

"Looking into all that licensing stuff. She spoke bureaucratese from all her years in banking, and she dearly loved research. It was such a good idea, we all thought. And that delightful young woman at the library, Susan Bingham, was helping her with it. It would have been so wonderful if Lorretta had found some way to cut expenses in the Medical Center. Now I'm not sure there's anyone with her expertise to carry on. Cammy might have been able to from her background in medicine, but all those years as an X-ray technician gave her cancer. She was only sixty-seven when she died." Two small tears trickled down Min's pug nose. "Forgive me, I'm still not over it." She wiped away her tears and took another bite of the aspic. There was silence at the table for a few moments.

Then Lucia asked, "Is there anyone at the Medical Center that we could talk to? Dr. Fuller refuses. It would need to be a person who's been there for a while and who will keep our conversation confidential. Someone not too close to the administration. Someone we can trust."

"That would be Scottie. She keeps swearing she's going to quit, but she says she just can't leave us. I went to her when I broke my ankle. She is just a dear. I have her to dinner every now and then. She's just a darling girl, and I wouldn't be a bit surprised if she was a friend of Dorothy's."

"Dorothy Hoffman?" Amy asked dubiously.

"I'll explain later," Lucia said.

"It's all right. I've gotten much braver about the word lesbian. You may say it. It means a homosexual, Amy, a friend of Dorothy from the Wizard of Oz. I'm not sure how it came about, but it's a common code phrase."

"Oh," Amy said, not quite understanding.

"Could I use your phone? Or, better, would you be willing to ask Scottie to come down here to look at your ankle or something? It might be better if no one knew she was talking to us. We aren't well liked by the administrators here," Lucia requested.

"How exciting. I'd be delighted to." She stood to go to the phone. Min sat next to the phone and dialed. "Is Scottie Tallese there? Good," she said. Then she put her hand on the receiver. "She's there and not busy with a patient. We're in luck." She paused, removing her hand from the receiver. "Hello, dear. This is Min Worthington. My ankle is throbbing, and I'm afraid I may have reinjured it. Do you have time to drop by and check it out? It would be so uncomfortable to walk over, and I hate being wheeled around in a chair. Thank you so much. That would be wonderful." She hung up the phone. "She'll be right over."

Scottie Tallese was a tall, willowy blonde in her late twenties with laughing blue eyes and a firm jaw. Her clothes looked like a tennis outfit of white blouse and shorts trimmed with lime green. "Who are your visitors, Min? Aren't these the infamous relatives of Margaret Traeger here to set Heritage House on its ear?"

"Well, yes, I guess we are," Amy said. "I'm Amy Traeger and this is Detective Lucia Ramos."

"Hi. I'm Scottie Tallese," she said, closing the door. "How's the ankle, Min?" Scottie walked over to her chair and knelt down.

"I'm a little embarrassed, Scottie. What I told you about my ankle was a fib. These girls wanted to talk to you without anyone knowing, so I just made it up to get you over here. I hope you aren't mad. It was quite wicked of me." Min's eyes sparkled as she looked at Scottie. It seemed to Lucia that Scottie's hand stayed on Min's knee a trifle longer than necessary. Lucia looked at Amy and raised her right eyebrow. Amy smiled and gave a slight nod. She had noticed it too.

"What's all this cloak and dagger stuff? I feel like I'm having dinner at the Mystery Playhouse in Mobile." Scottie got to her feet and faced Lucia and Amy.

"We'd like to talk about the medical center, if you're willing?" Amy asked.

"And we'd like our conversation to be kept confidential. Can you do that?" Lucia asked.

"Yes to both questions. But I still don't understand why it's so secret. I don't know anything important, I'm sure."

"We're not sure there's any reason to be secretive, but an unpleasant experience yesterday has made us cautious," Amy said.

"The snake in your car," Scottie offered.

"Yes. How did you hear about it?" Lucia asked.

"Jannie Anvil, the medical center secretary. Bubba Cook is her brother. He came over last night to have a beer with Jannie's husband Archie. He spent all evening laughing about the water snake you thought was a cottonmouth. She said he kept saying, 'And it wasn't even loaded,' and laughing himself silly. These Cajuns are a rowdy lot."

"Cajun? Sheriff Cook is a Cajun?"

"Sure. Most everybody from around Citronelle is Cajun. Why, they even had a third school system for them before integration. Some judge in the early thirties decided they weren't black, which, of course, they aren't, but he didn't think they were white either, cuz they had too much Indian blood in them. So he decided they were a third race—Cajun. Isn't that weird? People sure thought stupid things back then." She shook her blond curls in disbelief as she sat on the floor next to Min.

"Is there anyone in this county Sheriff Cook isn't related to?" Lucia asked, dismayed.

"Probably not, unless they moved in in the last ten years or they work at the hospital. They bring in a lot of people from outside the county to work there."

"You don't mean the medical center here at Heritage House?"

"Oh, no. I mean the State Hospital for the Insane. It used to be just for Negroes, but now any poor person can get sent there. They do a lot of drug and alcohol rehab stuff. I've been trying to get a job over there for years."

"You don't like working here?" Amy asked.

"I love the residents. But it's gotten pretty bad in terms of the staff."

"What do you mean, 'bad'?" Lucia asked, taking notes.

"Well, when I came to work here three-and-a-half years ago there were eighteen people working in the medical center. Now there are only nine. I end up having to give patients baths and all sorts of things. I work six days a week, and I'm on call twenty-four hours a day, seven days a week. I'm on a monthly salary so I don't get overtime. It's pretty tough. I don't have much of a life outside of work. Sam Pettigrew, he's the director, he says it's because of the lawsuit over Roman Craig's death. I haven't been allowed to use the therapeutic pool since he died." Her face looked mournful.

"How did he die?" Amy asked.

"He was a wheelchair patient, so he had to be put in a lift and be lowered into the pool. Michele, she was the aide working with him, had him over the pool but not in yet when her beeper went off. Mrs. Gatskill was having a seizure. By the time she got back, Mr. Craig had fallen out of the chair and drowned. I guess Michele forgot the seat-belt, even though she swore she didn't. Anyway, his family is suing for buckets of money, and so now they say we don't have enough money to hire anybody."

"Have there been other deaths at the medical center?" Lucia asked.

"Sure. There are lots of old people here. We have one or two a month. Mostly their hearts. Even Mrs. Batchelder, who had cancer, died of a heart attack. Doc Fuller said she couldn't tolerate the chemo."

Min chimed in, "And Joyce Corbett died when she fell off her balcony," Min offered. "It was very odd, because the balconies have very high railings. She had to have kind of boosted herself over. But you should talk to Dr. Roberts about that one. He came over to declare her dead, since Dr. Fuller was away. All of us in the Friday bridge club thought it very odd because it turned out she was despondent. Dr. Fuller had prescribed antidepressants, that Prozac stuff that can make you kill people, even yourself. None of us had any idea she was depressed, not even Edith Malone, and she was very good friends with Joyce. It was all so terrible." Min looked quite sad.

"Did Sheriff Cook investigate either death?" Lucia asked.

"Why, I guess so. I don't really know. Do you know, Scottie?"

"He investigated Mr. Craig's. I know because I had to give a deposition that I had trained Michele properly in the use of the lift and had shown her how to use the seatbelt. I don't know about Mrs. Corbett. I didn't know her."

"Have there been any other suspicious deaths at Heritage House since you've been here?" Lucia asked.

"Not really."

"Thank you very much, Ms. Tallese. Can I call you later if I have more questions?"

"Sure. My number is 999-5340. Leave a message. But you know who you should really talk to?" Scottie offered.

"Who?" Lucia asked.

"Mrs. Dexter. She was fired just after I got here. She might know a lot because she ran the medical center before Doc Fuller came. She lives in Mobile now and works at the Methodist Elder Care Center. We have lunch every now and then. Tell her I said you were okay. Otherwise she won't talk. Things got pretty nasty when they fired her. But she should tell you about that."

"Thank you for your help, Min, and the delicious lunch," Amy said.

"Anything I can do to help. Just ask." Min ushered them all out the door.

"Amy, how safe do you feel with the internal switchboard here?" Lucia asked as they walked down the carpeted hallway.

"Not very, not anymore. Are you thinking what I think you're thinking?"

"Yep. Let's head for town. We can use the pay phone at the Exxon station."

Lucia rolled down her window and left the door open a few moments before sliding in. Amy had already started the engine and switched the air conditioner to maximum.

"I guess there wasn't a bomb wired to the ignition. Do you think we should have checked in the glove compartment for scorpions?" Lucia teased.

"They probably wouldn't be 'loaded,'" Amy snarled a bit.

"You have to admit 'the snake isn't loaded' is a pretty funny comment." They both laughed.

"A lot funnier today than it was yesterday. Ah, with time you gain perspective," Amy philosophized.

"So how come all old people aren't smart?" Lucia asked.

"So how come it took us forever to catch on to the scam going on here? Everybody told us Lorretta was killed for money. The money she was most interested in was her own. The rates were tripled in a short amount of time when they should be going down. Lorretta's bookcase is full of books indicating that she was studying the financial management of this kind of place. All the pieces were there for us to see. Damn, we were so blind!" Amy was keeping both eyes on the road.

"From the outside, it looks good. People we respect decided to live here. The director is even an ex-priest. It's like an abusive family; when you like people you don't want to find something wrong with how they are living their lives."

"Damn, Rex Fletcher is the slimiest salesman this side of a California used car lot. If we had paid attention to our feelings, we would have started the investigation with him instead of getting sidetracked by the Friday bridge club. It's just that I'm so used to arrogance and officiousness from administrators of any sort that he seemed to be perfectly natural." She pounded her hand on the steering wheel.

"Well, you've got to admit, criminals hiding in a bureaucracy is perfect. You'd never notice them."

"We were so stupid." Amy tried to keep her attention on the road.

"Hold on there. We're not omniscient. We followed up on everything we knew. We just didn't know about the funny business finances of Heritage House."

"And the deaths! My god, how many people do you think they've killed?"

"That's jumping pretty far and pretty fast, Amy. We don't know they killed anyone, although it does seem really likely that Lorretta was killed by someone with access to a strong dosage of digitalis...."

"Dr. Fuller, probably," Amy said, turning to look at Lucia.

"Keep looking at the road, please. This is a bad time for us to end up in the hospital. We need to report what we've learned. If there's embezzlement, it's going to take someone who knows a lot more than we do to find it. But if there is embezzlement, I'll bet my last dollar someone in the administration of Heritage House killed Lorretta to cover it up.

Probably others too. But what motive do you think they could possibly have for causing those other deaths?"

"Money. When someone dies, Heritage House gets to keep all the money they paid for their apartment and then sell the apartment again to someone new."

Lucia was astounded. "You mean they paid more than the monthly fee?"

Amy nodded. "The apartments were sold like a condominium. Once you've bought in, you're in for life. As your health deteriorates you move into the medical center. And when you die, your apartment reverts to Heritage House. Your apartment isn't part of your estate."

"So everyone who dies means a profit to them."

"Yes, although I certainly never thought of it like that when I was reading the brochure. I thought of elderly people dying at the end of a long, expensive illness that would wipe out their savings. That idea terrified Maggie and, frankly, it scares me."

"What scares me is a lot of deaths in the same place and almost no thorough investigation of any of them," Lucia commented.

"Do you think the sheriff is in on it?" Amy shot an involuntary glance in the rearview mirror.

Lucia shrugged. "Maybe. It would be very convenient. I think it would be better to assume he is. You know, better safe than sorry."

Amy pulled into the Exxon station and parked next to the telephone. "So whom do we call?"

"I guess Byrd. I'm pretty sure we can trust him. And the feds. If there's any chance the local police are corrupt, they're the next in line. Or the state police, I guess. I haven't worked much with either one. But let's start with Byrd. Maybe you should pull the car behind the garage where it won't be so obvious."

"Good idea," Amy said, turning back toward the car. It only took her a minute to move the car into the dubious shelter of the service station's white stucco garage. Lucia followed her to the phone booth. Amy put her calling card on the broiling hot metal shelf under the phone and dialed Byrd's number from memory. She quickly explained what they had discovered in their conversation with Minerva and Scottie. Then she listened for a moment.

"Certainly, Mr. Byrd, but I'm sure we can get evidence." There was a longer pause in Amy's speech. "Let me talk to Lucia." She put her hand over the phone. "He says that it's probably not admissable. Do you think we can get something to back it up?"

"I think it's a bad idea. We should turn everything we know over to a law enforcement agency and let them do their job."

"Let's not keep him holding while we talk about it," Amy said. "We can call him back." She took her hand away from the phone and explained to Byrd that they would discuss it and call him, then hung up.

"Let's drive," Amy said. "I'm uncomfortable just standing around here. Besides, it's too hot!"

They got back in the Skylark and drove south.

"So, are we going back to Mobile?" Lucia asked.

"Not really. I'm just driving anywhere, nowhere." She switched the air conditioner on maximun. "Byrd called it sheer conjecture and gossip because we don't have a shred of hard evidence to back it up!"

"What do we have? An elderly woman, despondent..."

"Says Fuller, who's in with them," Amy retorted.

"We have no proof that she was pushed. No proof that the guy who was drowned didn't fall into the pool by accident. There's no hard evidence of anything and the circumstantial evidence is very thin. No judge would ever admit it."

"So, let's go get the hard evidence," Amy said, turning the car around. The car behind her honked. The driver made a rude gesture as he drove by.

"Park somewhere. I'd like your full attention on this discussion," Lucia ordered.

Obediently, Amy turned into the drive of an abandoned farmhouse. She pulled into the tall grass of what had been the front yard. "Let's stay in the car. This place looks full of snakes."

"Fine, but leave the air conditioning on."

"Why shouldn't we investigate the administration like we did the bridge club?" Amy asked.

"It's a lot more dangerous. We're talking about a whole group of people possibly killing for profit, not a scared elderly couple without any backup. Now we're the scared couple without backup. It's just plain dumb, Amy." Lucia startled when a huge grasshopper landed on the hood with a thump.

"If we turn it over to law enforcement, will they do the investigation or will they blow it off?" There was an accusatory note in Amy's voice.

"I can't guarantee anything, Amy. We're associated with the defense in a murder investigation. They may figure it's a smoke screen designed to get Maggie off."

"Then we have to investigate." Amy pulled back to the drive.

"Neither of us is Rambo. These people don't hesitate to kill, Amy. I really think we need backup. This isn't a TV show where you know the stars aren't going to die until the end of the season."

"Okay," Amy said, "We'll call Byrd. Tell him to hire some gun-toting private investigator. Will that be more sensible?" she asked, pulling back onto the highway.

"I guess," Lucia said, not sounding very reassured.

The station attendant gave them a quizzical look as they drove back into the Exxon station again. Amy parked behind the garage. Lucia hopped out into the heat and jogged over to the phone. She dialed Byrd's number. When Roz answered, Lucia quickly repeated her concerns and asked if Byrd's office could send backup. She covered the mouthpiece with her hand and asked Amy to get her notebook and pen. She nodded several times and wrote the name of the investigator in her notebook. "Okay," she said to the phone. "We'll meet him at Ms. Traeger's apartment. Do you have that address and phone? Good." She said goodbye and hung up. "Back to the apartment," she said to Amy as they walked to the rental car.

"I don't feel terribly safe there. Why don't we stop at the desk on our way in and get nosy? We might find out something interesting, and we'll be in a place too public for anyone to harm us." Amy slid into the driver's seat.

"Why not?" Lucia agreed, taking the passenger side. She began to think out loud as she took notes. "Doc Fuller. Why would a doctor work in a job a physician's assistant could handle? Why would Heritage House pay a doctor when someone cheaper would do? Sam Pettigrew. Why leave the priesthood? That's an interesting question, isn't it?" she asked Amy.

"I think so."

"Fletcher, what's his background? How did all these men end up together in a retirement complex in southern Alabama? What's the link? It should be easy enough to track the doctor. Licensing records are easy to get at. I wonder if he's a doctor at all."

"That's why Lorretta had all those financial textbooks. She was checking on the financial picture at Heritage House. How could we have been so blind?" She pounded the dash with her left hand. "Damn. There's bound to be proof of embezzlement. You can't hide that forever."

"You can destroy records. Embezzlement isn't murder. I don't know how we can prove they're linked. Here's the turn." Lucia braced herself for the braking Amy would have to do to make the turn.

Amy made the turn sharply but competently, pulled up in front of the entrance, and parked. "Shall we brave the lion in his den, Officer Ramos?" she asked, almost leaping from the Skylark.

Lucia didn't bother to answer as she followed Amy to the reception desk. The receptionist wasn't in the small office. Amy slapped the counter bell several times. The plump, cheerful attendant ambled through the door at the back of the office.

"Hold your horses. I'm coming." She smiled genially. "Had to visit the little girl's room. What can I do for you ladies?"

"I need a copy of my aunt's billing record," Amy improvised.

"Well, now, I heard that bell dinging away and I figured this place was on fire. You just need your bill?" She maintained her tone of good humor as she rested her elbows on the counter.

"The lawyer said he needed it right away," Amy assured her.

"Too bad. Can't do it. All the papers are kept over at the Farm."

"The Farm?" Lucia asked.

"Heritage Farm. It's about four miles from here as the crow flies. That's where all the business is done for the Acres. You won't find anyone there, though. They all went down to Mobile for a meeting with the church folks."

Lucia and Amy exchanged glances. "How do we get there?" Lucia asked. "We'd love to see it."

"Well, you could just walk down the bridle path. It'd take you about an hour or so. It's all Heritage land. But if you're in a hurry, you'd probably better drive." She pointed a pudgy finger to the right. "Down the highway about three miles, then left down Oakhill Road for about another three. You'll see a big horse-shaped sign, says 'Heritage Hot Bloods.' They used to breed racehorses, but they've pretty much sold it off. Just kept a few easy mares for the folks to ride. Mr. Pettigrew rides over here a couple of times a week. There's three or four residents who ride too."

"Thanks." Amy grabbed Lucia's hand and pulled her away. "Come on, Lucia. We need to get back to Citronelle to pick up those papers. We can call for the billing records from there." She almost ran to the door.

"What papers?" Lucia whispered.

"Later." Amy tore down the front steps at breakneck speed. She was in the car and had it turned on by the time Lucia got to the bottom stair.

"What papers?" Lucia repeated as she fastened her seat belt.

"None. I just said that to throw them off, in case the receptionist is in with them." Amy accelerated. "We're going to Heritage Farm. It's our best chance to check everything out."

"Amy, you're really sure about all this, aren't you? If you're suggesting breaking and entering, I'm out. I can't go along with that." Lucia sounded alarmed.

"No, just hoping that they've left a low-level flunky with no imagination in charge. I don't know. It's probably stupid, but I hope we can use the needing-a-bill story to get a look at the files. Pretty farfetched, huh?" She took her eyes off the road for a moment to look at Lucia pleadingly.

"I guess it sounds okay. I just wish we had backup."

"Me too." Amy slowed the car. "Help me find Oakhill Road." She drove almost half a mile farther before Lucia spotted the road sign. The motorist behind her ignored her left turn signal and pulled out to pass. "Idiot," Amy commented.

The horse-shaped sign was very obvious. It was slightly larger than life-size. The posts were placed behind the legs of the horse silhouette and 'Heritage Hot Bloods' was written across the body of the brown horse. The nose of the sign seemed to point down the narrow country lane. It was a well-maintained gravel road that Amy turned on to. White wood fences bordered either side. Occasionally, a white fence would run perpendicular to the road, dividing the fields.

"This reminds me of that subdivision that Freddie Christian lives on. No houses here, though. This place is huge. I guess if it's owned by churches, they don't have to pay property taxes on it. Must cost a fortune to keep up, though."

On the left the fields gave way to pine woods with scrub underneath the boughs. A slight knoll blocked the view on the right. Amy slowed down.

"Do you think we should park out of sight and try to sneak up?"

"No breaking and entering," Lucia reminded her.

"We go up to the front door and knock."

"Right," Lucia agreed.

The nouveau plantation house appeared on the right. It was considerably smaller than Heritage House, but still imposing. There were several outbuildings scattered about the grounds. No one seemed stirring at any one of them. Amy slowed to a stop in front of the entrance steps. Lucia noticed that the portico had rose plants in boxes. The shading went from pink to white.

Amy took a deep breath. "Shall we?"

"Barge in where angels fear to tread? Why not?" Lucia responded, opening her door. The steps were wood rather than marble, as were the columns. Amy rang the doorbell. There was a long wait. She shrugged and tried again.

"Maybe we should give up," Lucia suggested.

The door swung open before Amy could reply. The smile on Rex Fletcher's homely face disappeared immediately.

"What are you doing here? This is private property. Get out of here. We're having a meeting."

"Yes, I know," Amy extemporized. "We thought the churches might be interested to know what we've learned about the financial situation at Heritage House. We've turned up some interesting information that they should be made aware of."

"For example?" Sam Pettigrew asked from behind Rex. His furrowed brow emphasized his dark brown eyes. He did not look pleased.

"About the expenses in the medical center. About cuts in staff and increases in charges," Amy replied, ignoring Lucia's grimace.

"Shit. We can't let them talk to the preachers, Sam."

"Correct," Pettigrew agreed. He reached inside his suit coat and withdrew a small revolver. Lucia took a sharp breath. Pettigrew handed the gun to Rex. "Don't botch this like you did the snake. Take them out to the stable and lock them in the hay room. We'll deal with them later."

Rex did as he was ordered, motioning the women out the door.

"Take them through the house, idiot," Pettigrew snarled. "What if one of the ministers comes early and sees you marching them along at gunpoint? Come to think of it, I should move their car. No point in leaving loose ends about. The keys, Miss Traeger." He held out his well-manicured hand. Amy dropped the keys into his palm. He gestured down the central hallway. Amy and Lucia stepped past him.

"No screw-ups, Rex," he warned, as he stepped out the front door.

Fletcher hustled them down the hall. Lucia looked at each closed door with hope but no expectation. None opened. They exited the mansion from the back and walked across the gravel drive. Several expensive cars were parked near the back entrance. Lucia winced. If only they had been parked in the front. Rex prodded her in the back with the twenty-two revolver. She hurried her pace, drawing even with Amy.

"I guess we were right about the money," Lucia said.

"Shut up, bitch, and walk faster. The barn's on the left."

His voice was as unpleasant as his face.

The temperature dropped slightly as they entered the darkness of the stable. Several horses sighted them through open stalls and nickered. "I'll feed you later, fatsos," Rex called to the mares.

They passed two closed doors. "Stop here," Rex ordered. He walked past them to open one of the doors. Lucia looked at Amy and nodded slightly.

Amy dropped to her knees and grabbed for his legs as Lucia tried to wrestle the gun from his hand. Startled and off balance, Rex fell into the partially open door. Just as Lucia almost gained control of the revolver, Pettigrew grabbed Amy from behind and pulled her to her feet.

Rex jerked the gun from Lucia and fired at her. The pain from the bullet penetrating her shoulder stopped her cold.

"Stop shooting, jerk-off. Some minister might be driving up and hear."

Rex paused for an instant, then slugged Amy across the side of the head. She slumped in Pettigrew's rough embrace. He kicked the door open wider and dragged her through it. "Get the other one in here," he snarled at Fletcher.

The pain from Rex's yank on her injured arm flooded Lucia with dizziness. She fell to her knees inside the hay room, barely noticing as they closed the door and slid home the outside bolt.

Lucia pressed her hand as hard as she could against her bleeding shoulder. The other arm didn't want to move.

"Damn. The first time I get shot and it isn't even covered by Worker's Comp," she thought, and began to giggle. "Shock. I'm in shock. Keep the victim warm. Try to breath deeply and regularly. I guess they weren't meeting in Mobile." Her weak left hand fumbled with a horse blanket that had been thrown over a bale of hay. She managed to pull it over herself as she snuggled against Amy's unconscious body. "She's still warm. She must be alive. She would be cold if she were dead," Lucia thought.

"Don't die," she whispered in Amy's unresponsive ear. "Don't die. Don't die," she chanted. Her body froze into a shell of pain. She refused to blink her eyes, afraid they wouldn't reopen. "Don't die, don't die," she repeated to herself as much as to Amy.

Flies began to buzz near Lucia's face. She began to be afraid that one would fly into her eyes. "Don't die," she wept. The tears washed the dryness out of her eyes. "Don't die," she whispered, unable to think of anything else to say.

Amy moaned. "God, my head hurts."

"Don't die, Amy."

"I'm not. Where are we? What happened?" She clenched her teeth against the pain.

"Hay room. They locked the door. I'm shot, Amy. Please do something." Lucia began to weep again. "I thought you were dead."

Very slowly Amy raised her head. "There's blood all over you," Amy said frantically. "Are you okay, querida?"

"No, I'm shot. It hurts a lot. I'm bleeding. I'm very dizzy."

"Let me see."

Lucia shook her head slightly. "I don't want to take my hand away. It'll bleed more."

Amy sat up very slowly. "We need a bandage." She lifted the bottom of her blouse up to her mouth and ripped it with her teeth. "Shit. That hurt." She reached down and took off her sandal, then her socks, which she rolled up into a ball. "I'm going to tie this over your wound. If I don't pass out first."

Her fingers were gentle as they moved Lucia's hand away from her shoulder. She put the ball of socks on top of the wound and pressed harder. Lucia screamed.

"I'm so sorry, Lucia." Amy stared at her bloody hand. Then she tied the socks in place with the strip of blouse. The blood seemed to stop flowing. Amy slowly stood up.

"I have to disassociate to make it through this, Lucita. It's very cold. I'll have no feeling at all. But have faith that when this is over, I can be myself again." Amy walked over to the locked door and examined it carefully. "The padlock is on the other side so I couldn't pick it, even if I knew how, which I don't." She seemed to be more talking out loud to herself than to Lucia. "There is a way out. There must be. All the walls are the same. Both sides of the door are not the same. Hinges." Amy turned to examine the other side of the door. "Yes. Hinges on the inside." She tugged at the top of the middle hinge pin. It didn't budge. "Screwdriver, nail, hammer. Forget it. Nothing but hay," Amy murmured.

Lucia lay still, watching Amy rove about the stall looking for a tool. Amy stood above her prone body and took inventory.

"No belt buckle, no hairpins, no knife. Of course. Change. Lucia, do you have change in your pocket?"

"Yes," Lucia said, reaching to get it. She moaned softly with the effort to move.

"No. I'll get it. You rest. You're going to need your strength." Amy slipped a hand in Lucia's pocket. She brought out a dime and three pennies. None of them would fit in the tiny crack between the bolthead and the hinge. "They're too fat," Amy said in a very young voice. Then it changed, became stronger. "There's something else, there has to be."

"Birkenstocks," Lucia said.

Amy looked at her feet. There were three buckles on each sandal. A huge grin crossed her face. "Yes. Perfect." The edge of the buckle fit in the cracks but didn't budge the bolt. "Hammer," Amy said. "Shoes, heel."

Lucia used the toe of one foot to slide off a black Stride Rite pump. Amy scooped it up in triumph. "Perfect, thanks."

The force of the blows bent the buckle, but not before the bolt head moved up. Amy switched to another buckle.

The bolt moved up enough to grasp. She twisted and pulled it up about two inches, but left it in place to keep pressure off the other hinges.

The bolt of the bottom hinge bent three buckles before it budged at all. It would not move beyond the first quarter of an inch. "Force, leverage," Amy muttered. A flicker of pain crossed her face as she stood from her stooped position. Her eyes inventoried the room again. "Baling wire," she said.

"That's right, mejita," Lucia encouraged. "You can fix anything with baling wire." Lucia didn't mention that she couldn't imagine how.

Amy wrapped one end of a length of wire around the bolt and tried to pull it. Nothing happened. She jerked. It didn't budge. She stared at it, her eyes narrowed with intense thought.

"Loop it over the pipe support in the wall, Amy," Lucia suggested.

Another piece of wire was twisted into the original to give it the length to go over the pipe. Amy put a loop in the end and put her foot through the loop. She held on to the pipe with both hands and shifted her weight onto her foot. She grimaced. The wire cut into her foot. The Birkenstock with one remaining buckle went back on her left foot. She tried again. The bolt moved slowly upward, then threw her off balance as it popped out.

Amy got up swiftly and tugged at the middle bolt. It came free. She eyed the top bolt, then shrugged. She lifted the lowest free corner. The door pivoted enough to leave a sizable opening.

"We're out of here," Lucia said trying to struggle to her feet without using her injured shoulder. "I'm too dizzy."

"Wait," Amy commanded. "Lie down with your head toward the door." Lucia complied. Amy grasped the material at the shoulders of Lucia's shirt and dragged her across the floor. She crawled through the tilted door, then turned to pull Lucia through. Lucia moaned with the pain of moving.

"Can you stand up?" Amy whispered.

"I can try."

Amy stood up and helped pull Lucia to her knees. "Wait," Lucia said. "I need a minute. I'm really dizzy." Amy counted to ten.

"Now?" she asked.

Lucia nodded. Amy bent until she was under Lucia's good arm. She pulled her to her feet. Very slowly, they began to walk down the center hall of the barn. The extra weight of Lucia's body threw Amy off balance. When her bare foot struck a rock, she stumbled and fell. Lucia shifted toward the wall next to her, making a tremendous clatter as she hit the metal panel. She began to hiccup.

"It's a good thing my head hurts too much to laugh or I'd be in hysterics," Amy muttered, getting to her feet. She eased herself under Lucia's shoulder and half carried her to the door leading to the pasture. The horses ignored her until she dumped some grain in the feeders. The sound of the metal cup hitting the feeders got their attention and five trotted over.

"Don't tell me you want us to ride out of here? Amy, this isn't a Western. I'm very dizzy. I don't think I could stay on a horse if my life depended on it." Lucia wiped the sweat off her forehead. The walk down the center of the barn had taken more effort than seemed possible. At least the sweat was a sign she wasn't in shock anymore.

"It does depend on it. We don't have car keys anyway and the cars are parked in full view of the main house. They would hear us if we tried to take the tractor. I think it's only about four miles to the apartments. I wish we could stop somewhere in between, but I'm afraid to trust anyone."

While talking she put a bridle on the most placid-looking mare. The saddle she threw over it looked like an English saddle with wing-like projections on the front.

"This is an Aussie saddle. It's easier to stay in than the others even though it's too big for you. I wish there were two."

"Couldn't we just go up to the front door and announce ourselves? They can't shoot us with all those people watching," Lucia pleaded.

"They might kill us and all those witnesses too. Do you want to risk it?" Amy asked, putting a bridle on a tall black mare.

"No, I guess not. When we get home I'm going to say a novena in gratitude because the way I figure it, it's going to take a miracle for me to stay on this horse." She patted her chestnut mount on the neck. "Nice horse. I think I'll call her Jude, the patron saint of impossible problems. Hey Jude, be nice to me, okay?" Lucia said nervously. "I haven't been on a horse in maybe twenty years. But if you do good, I'll buy you fifty pounds of oats."

Amy had finished saddling the black mare. She came back to check the girth on Lucia's horse. With a swift knee in the belly, she forced the horse to let out the air that had been swelling up. "Goddess, I hate to do that. But we don't have time to be gentle," she said quickly tightening the cinch. She did the same to her mount. "Time to go up, Lucia. Do you think you can do it?"

"Not a prayer."

Amy turned over a bucket next to the chestnut. "Stand on this and I'll hold the horse."

"I'll need a hand just to get on the bucket, much less the horse," Lucia retorted.

"Okay," Amy answered. She helped Lucia steady herself on the bucket bottom, then walked the chestnut up next to Lucia. Amy dropped the reins. The mare stood still without a muscle moving. "We're in luck. This horse ground-ties." Lucia maneuvered her left foot into the stirrup as Amy held her steady. She put both hands around Lucia's waist. "On the count of three, try to heave yourself up. Worry about your feet later."

Lucia did as she was instructed, moaning as the violent action tore open the wound on her shoulder. She swayed in the saddle.

"Put your head down on the horse's neck. It'll keep you more balanced. Don't worry, I'll lead your horse. Just stay on it. Do you hear me, Lucia?"

"Yes," Lucia whispered. "I'll try."

"Fuck 'try.' Do it! I'll lead your horse. You just have to stay on." Amy looped Lucia's reins through a ring on the back of the saddle on the black mare and mounted the horse. "Walk," she ordered it, squeezing gently with her legs. Both horses ambled off. Amy kept the barn between the main house and the horses until they were well into the pine woods. She constantly checked over her shoulder to be sure Lucia was still on.

Twice they had to follow wire fences until Amy found gates. Twice she dismounted to open the gates and led both horses through. She didn't bother to close them. Finally they hit the bridle path.

"I think it's about three miles to Heritage House now. Can you hang on?" she called back to Lucia.

"Yeah," Lucia grunted, not really believing it.

The pace picked up without all the underbrush to catch at them. Amy tried to trot, then slowed down when it was obvious that Lucia was close to falling out of the saddle.

A large branch, snapped off in the wind, had fallen across the path, forcing them to go even slower. Carefully the horses picked their way through the debris. Amy urged them to a faster walk once they were through. "Bodecia," she whispered to the horse. "That's what I'd name you. No matter what, you keep going. You never stop. Sweet girl, Bodecia." A soft nicker seemed to indicate the mare's approval.

When they got to the highway, Amy held the horses

back in the trees until the road was clear of traffic, then urged them across. Safely on the other side, she slowed to a walk. "It's not far now," she called back to Lucia.

"I know," Lucia whispered too low for Amy to hear. "I've been here before."

Amy fought the urge to break into a gallop. There was no way to know what kind of greeting awaited them at Heritage House. She pondered her options as the horses plodded on.

She stopped at the first glimpse of the building. "Kick your feet out of the stirrups. You're staying here." Amy dismounted.

"Right," Lucia said, not quite clear on where 'here' was. She did as she was ordered.

"Swing your right leg over and kind of slide down on your butt. I'll catch you."

Lucia tried to manage her leg, but the effort of swinging it unbalanced her and pitched her from the saddle into Amy's arms. Both fell to the ground. Amy paused, shaking her head to clear it, then scrambled to her knees. Locking her arms under Lucia's, she dragged her out of the bridle path into the bushes beside it.

"What now, my love?" Lucia croaked painfully.

"Now we send for the Marines," Amy said. The horses occupied themselves with munching the shrubbery as Amy crept through the trees to the back of the apartments. She picked up several fist-sized rocks and approached the window she hoped led to Maggie's apartment.

The first rock shattered a sizable hole in the middle of the window. Amy used another to knock out the shards stuck in the frame. She couldn't get out the small pieces held in place by molding. Shrugging, she stripped off her slacks and tossed them over the bottom edge just as an elderly woman stuck her head out of the window next door.

"What's going on?" she shrieked.

"A robbery. Call the state police and the FBI," Amy called back.

The woman slammed the window shut as Amy hoisted herself over the window ledge. She dashed for the phone and dialed 911. If the sheriff wasn't trustworthy, there were other options.

"911. What's your emergency?" The man on the other end demanded.

Amy didn't pause. "Terrible fire at the Heritage House in Mt. Vernon. Send an ambulance. Hurry. I've got to get out of here." She coughed for effect, then hung up. Paper towels draped over the burners on the stove caught fire quickly. Amy used tongs to toss them into the sink onto the towels she had crumpled in there to be burned. The smoke alarm went crazy.

She decided there was time enough to grab clothes from the bedroom. The smouldering fire had filled the apartment with smoke by the time she dressed. She checked to be sure it hadn't spread beyond the sink, but it was nicely contained.

People were already in the hall, milling about as she opened the door. "Fire," she screamed.

A woman on crutches pulled down the fire alarm in the hall as she passed it. Amy fell in behind her and joined the general exodus. She was panting by the time she returned to Lucia.

"My god, what did you do?" Lucia asked, glimpsing some of the chaos even from the hidden position.

"Fire alarm," Amy said, proudly watching the flocks of people pouring out of every door like ants scurrying from a disturbed den. The sound of sirens indicated that help was rapidly approaching. "Will you be okay while I flag down an ambulance?"

"Sure," Lucia murmured. She had grown used to the current level of pain. As long as she didn't move, it was bearable.

Amy returned with two strong young men and a stretcher. "Gently," she said to them as they tried to slide the back board under Lucia. It stuck in the bushes and delayed the procedure.

"It's not my back, it's my shoulder," Lucia said. "I think I can sit up if that would help."

"Don't move," the redhead ordered curtly. "We gotta do it right. We don't want to hurt you." They finally got the board in place. Next came the neck brace. Lucia rolled her eyes.

"I'm going to bleed to death by the time you get me in the ambulance," she commented.

"No fresh blood on that rag you got tied on your shoulder and your blood pressure is fine. We've got plenty of time to do it right," the redhead responded.

Behind his back and out of his sight, Amy shrugged. This was the help she had sent for and she wasn't about to argue with him.

They finally got Lucia wrapped in a blanket and strapped to the stretcher. The redhead put an IV of saline solution into a vein in her good arm. He tucked the plastic bag of solution next to Lucia's face and motioned for his partner to pick up the other end of the stretcher. They carried her to the waiting ambulance. Amy followed them inside.

"Hey, you can't come in here," the redhead yelled at her.

"I suffered a bad blow to the head. I need transportation to the hospital too."

"Where on your head?" he asked suspiciously. Amy put her hand on the sizable knot that had formed on the left of her skull. He reached out to feel it and let out a whistle.

"That's a humdinger, all right. Let me check your eyes." He shown a tiny flashlight into her pupils. "I think you're going to be okay, but we'll let the docs check you out anyway. Please lie down right here on that stretcher. I need to strap you in for the ride."

His partner was pulling the ambulance out of the drive as the redhead tucked the blanket around Amy. Despite the heat, it was oddly comforting. For the first time in two days, Amy felt safe. She closed her eyes and took a deep, cleansing breath. Before she could exhale, the young man shook her gently.

"Don't go to sleep, ma'am. It's a real bad idea with head injuries. You need to stay awake and alert."

"That isn't easy when you're bone-tired and you're lying down." Amy yawned.

"Come on, Amy, wake up," Lucia yelled at her.

"Okay, okay, but somebody needs to entertain me," she replied.

"Well, ma'am, I sure would like to know what's going on. Like who set the place on fire and who shot this woman here and all." Avid curiosity glistened in his eyes.

"It's a long story. It started with a woman being poisoned last Sunday...."

Twenty minutes later, Amy finished her account. Her voice was raspy with the effort.

"We're almost to the hospital now, if you want to stop talking. It sure was interesting. I hope your aunt comes out okay. If there's anything I can do to help..."

"The horses!" Amy yelped. "I forgot the horses. I didn't even take their saddles off. Would you find them? It's much too close to the highway for them to be loose." Her face was stricken at the thought of her neglect of their saviors. The young man patted her awkwardly on the shoulder, then checked Lucia's and her vital signs one last time.

"It'll be fine, ma'am. I'll call my brother Daryl. He lives a couple of miles south of Calvert. He'll check on them, but I'm sure they're home eating hay by now. Don't you worry none. They'll be just fine. We're here now, at the emergency room. They'll take good care of you." He stood up and threw open the back doors of the ambulance. Two young women were waiting for him, each standing by a gurney.

He stepped out of the way to let the black woman into the ambulance. She rapidly checked pulse and blood pressure in both patients. "How do you feel?" she asked.

"Shitty," Lucia said.

"Horrible. My head is throbbing," Amy replied.

"Take the shoulder wound first," she said, gesturing at Lucia. "Let me check your eyes." She moved into the cab for a moment while the two men and the other woman slid Lucia onto the gurney and through the ambulance doors.

"I'm not sure what the admissions procedures are, but we'd like a private room together. My attorney, Andrew Byrd, can vouch for my fiscal solvency. I've no idea where either of our insurance cards are, but we're both insured," Amy said. As the young woman leaned over to check her pupils, Amy read her name tag. "Thank you, Dr. Vann."

"I haven't done anything yet, but you're welcome." She moved a pen in front of Amy's face. "Watch the end of the pen. Good. What day is it today?"

"I've rather lost track in the excitement. Let's see, we flew in on Monday, the arraignment was on Wednesday. This must be Thursday."

"Good. Who is the President?"

"A stooge of the rich who is about to leave office, replaced by President Barbara Boxer."

Dr. Nicole Vann gave a deep, hearty laugh. "Well, I guess I know who you're voting for in November. That counts as a right answer in my book." She felt Amy's scalp tenderly over the lump. "Your head was banged pretty good, but you're all right and your eyes are fine. I'd like to do a series of skull X-rays, maybe an MRI. I'll see what I can do on a room."

"The director of Mobile General Hospital knows us." Amy crossed her fingers.

"A friend of Frances, huh? Well, this is her hospital, so I guess you'll get a VIP room." Dr. Vann patted her on the arm. "Relax. Everything is going to be fine."

The procedures dragged out for hours, but in the end Amy got her way. She and Lucia lay on beds next to each other. The open back of the hospital gown felt terribly vulnerable to Amy but everything else seemed safe. The pain in her head began to recede. She poked her spoon at the red jello a young aide had brought. Lucia snored gently.

"Bored with the food already?" asked a gorgeous grey-haired woman in a mauve business suit. Her laughing blue eyes assessed Amy thoroughly. "I'm Helen Frances. There are easier ways to meet me than getting yourself admitted to my facility, you know."

Amy smiled and extended her hand. "Amy Traeger. It's lovely to meet you. How are we really?"

"Fine. You can trust your doctors. I picked them myself. I'd have to answer to Freddie Christian if anything happened to you, so I was very careful. You have a mild concussion, no fracture, no bleeding. Lucia Ramos is a bit more seriously injured, but nothing dangerous. The bullet lodged against the shoulder blade. A twenty-two doesn't have a lot of power. The bone has a hairline fracture from the impact. The surgeon got the bullet out and sewed her up very tidily. She probably won't even have a scar. Infection is the real worry with bullet wounds like this, so the doctor prescribed a heavy dose of antibiotics. We have her medical records from San Antonio."

"You do?" Amy asked in amazement.

"Freddie Christian was my first call. She has an amazing number of friends. With her help and a fax machine we had them in less than an hour." Ms. Frances made a thumbs-up gesture. "So everything is fine. I have to go, but if you need anything the staff should be very cooperative. Your aunt is waiting to see you. Are you up to it?"

A huge grin broke across Amy's face. "Absolutely. And thanks for everything."

"Don't thank me, thank Freddie." She left the room but held the door open for Maggie. Tears streaked Maggie's face. Her hands trembled as her fingers searched Amy's face for signs of injury. They lingered for a moment on a small scratch from a branch.

"Are you really all right, dear Amy? I will never forgive myself that you were injured trying to clear my name."

"Traeger, get off it." Ruby's voice boomed from her diminutive body in the doorway. She was carrying Amy's overnight bag.

"Yes, Maggie, get off it. None of this is your fault. Got it?" Amy asked fiercely. She kissed Maggie's fingertip, then clasped her hand.

Maggie nodded. "We can't stay long. The rules had to be bent for us to visit at all. Helen Frances is certainly a lovely woman. She's been so cooperative."

"A knock-out in the looks department too. Is she single?" Ruby asked, putting the overnight bag on a shelf of Amy's nightstand.

Amy shrugged as Maggie said, "You're not. How's Lucia, Amy? Is she really all right?"

"Yes, she is. They gave her a painkiller and she went right to sleep. Frankly, I'm ready to join her. Give me a goodnight kiss and toss this jello in the toilet, please." Maggie brushed Amy's forehead with her lips.

"Safe rest and sweet dreams." Maggie moved the tray table to the side of the bed and picked up the offending jello. "We put a few things in your bag for you and Lucia. Oh, and the sheriff is outside waiting to see you. What should I tell him?"

"Tell him to go suck a snake. I'm going to sleep." Amy closed her eyes and tried to snuggle into the bed without moving her pounding head.

"Goodnight, child. Sleep tight," Ruby's voice said. The lights went out.

"I should have called Tía Luz," Amy thought as she drifted off to sleep. She drowsed through several blood pressure checks during the night and early morning.

Tía Luz was her first thought in the morning when she was awakened by the clatter of the cart carrying the breakfast trays. Amy checked Lucia, who was still sleeping, then put through her call to San Antonio. Luz had already heard from Freddie Christian. She told Amy that the Police Department also knew about the shooting and didn't expect Lucia back until she was well. Luz had talked to Lucia's surgeon and was able to reassure Amy about Lucia's condition.

"Relax, Amy. She'll be fine. You two take some time. Go stay on a beach somewhere and rest. Senora Christian also called your office. There's nothing to worry about." Luz's voice flowed like balm over Amy's jangled nerves.

She checked the sleeping Lucia again before taking a shower. The hot water felt very soothing on her aching head. She lathered her scalp, carefully avoiding the throbbing lump. She smiled as she pulled on the yellow sundress that her aunt had packed for her. Maggie was always trying to get Amy to wear more dresses.

Feeling almost human, Amy emerged from the bathroom just as a young woman in a pink-and-white-striped uniform pushed a cart into the room. She smiled tentatively at Amy. "Are you a visitor?" she asked, obviously confused by the lack of hospital clothes on Amy's body.

"No. I'm the patient in that bed." Amy gestured to the empty one near the windows. "I hope that isn't more jello."

"You're on a regular diet, aren't you?" The young woman's blue eyes blinked with alarm.

"Sure. Just leave it on my table."

"Coffee," Lucia croaked weakly. "Quick."

"Right away," the young woman said, pouring a steady

stream into the thick white cup on Lucia's tray. "I'll be back in about half an hour for the empties."

Lucia tried to sit up. She didn't make it. "Jesus y Mariá. Was I hit by a truck? I feel like shit, Amy."

Amy moved the pad that controlled the bed onto the side of Lucia's good arm. "You have a very small but very nasty hole through a lot of muscle in your shoulder. I'm told it will heal nicely and may not even leave a scar." She pressed buttons moving the bed up in various places until Lucia indicated that she was more or less comfortable. She nodded gratefully as Amy handed her the coffee cup.

Amy discovered there wasn't a lock on the door, then pulled a chair in front of it. "Time for my examination of the patient." She bent over Lucia and pulled off the covers.

"Let me know what you find," Lucia teased.

"Toes, in much better shape than mine." Amy kissed them, each in turn. "Ankle, seems good; other is also fine." Each brown ankle was grazed by Amy's lips. Gradually, she worked her way up Lucia's body, pausing at each bruise or scratch.

"My thighs are awfully sore from that horse. They could use a lot of kissing," Lucia said wistfully.

Amy complied, then moved higher, checking carefully to see that Lucia's dark tight curls covered no injuries. She covered her dark triangle with kisses before moving onto Lucia's belly.

Small whimpering sounds came from Lucia's throat. "Am I hurting you?" Amy asked solicitously.

"Not yet. Come to think of it, I don't hurt a bit. But do keep checking." Lucia began to flex her thighs.

"Yes." Amy moved up to her breasts. She moved her lips in a circle around each breast and then kissed Lucia's hard nipples.

"You know, someone could walk in at any second," Lucia commented as desire began to warm her groin.

"Yes," Amy said, moving her lips to Lucia's collarbone.

She kissed very carefully around the bandage. She didn't comment on the reddish brown stain. She kissed down the length of Lucia's unwounded arm.

At that moment, there was a knock on the door. "Damn," Amy muttered as she flipped the sheet and light blanket back into position. "Just a minute," she called out. She removed the chair and opened the door.

"The sheriff from Tensaw County insists on seeing you, Miz Ramos, Miz Traeger." The worried look etched out-of-place lines on the young black face.

"Tell him to come in," Amy said. Relief spread through his face as he nodded. He obviously felt more comfortable saying yes than no to a man in uniform. "That okay with you, Lucia?"

"Sure," she replied, shrugging only one shoulder.

Sheriff Beauford Cook appeared at the door in full uniform. He removed his hat and held it in his hands. "Ladies," he said, then paused.

"Yes," Amy prompted. "Are you here to arrest me for arson?"

"No, ma'am," he said emphatically. "Well, I, ah..."

"False fire alarm?" she asked.

"Amy, let the man talk," Lucia urged gently.

"I came to apologize." The words came out in almost a whisper. His voice grew stronger. "I was so sure Miz Traeger was guilty, I never paid no attention to anything else. I almost got you two killed with my plumb stupidity and I'm real ashamed of myself. I came to ask your pardon." He hung his head like a contrite child.

"You did your job the best way you knew how. No one can do more than that," Lucia responded.

"But that wasn't good enough. It got a good police officer shot. I came to ask your forgiveness, Officer Ramos."

"Of course you're forgiven," Lucia said. Amy nodded her agreement.

"Thank you, ladies. I appreciate it." He lifted his head

in relief. "I reckon you'd like an update. The firefighters called me after they let you off. I went over to Heritage Farms with half a dozen of my men. We sat around and waited until all the ministers left, then drove up and arrested the lot of them crooks and murderers as pretty as you please.

"Turned out they was being investigated by the IRS anyway. They all got records. That whiney little snake Fletcher is singing like a canary bird for a reduced sentence on your assault, Officer Ramos. Seems like he and Pettigrew killed half a dozen old folks before they poisoned Miz Millett."

"My god, you got him to confess to those murders?" Amy exclaimed.

"Yes, ma'am. Alabama has the death penalty and attempted murder of an officer of the law is a capital offense. We had him cold on that one so he pled down to accessory. He won't be leaving prison until he's a very old man. Pettigrew will get the death penalty. Fuller is an addict. Spent some time in a Montana prison. He'll plea-bargain."

"Sounds good," Lucia commented.

"What about my aunt?" Amy asked.

"All charges have been dropped. I done apologized to her already. I'm real sorry I was such a horse's ass about that snake. Turns out Fletcher thought it was a moccasin, too. It was real tasty, though. The missus said to say thanks for the snake. Well, I gotta go." He solemnly shook both Lucia's and Amy's hands and left. Amy burst out laughing as soon as the door closed.

"It wasn't loaded, but it was real tasty. This is too much. I can't believe he apologized. I never expected that!"

"That took guts. He turned out to be pretty decent after all. I guess Reynolds isn't going to be too mad at me except for getting shot. He's going to chew me out for not having backup. 'This isn't a schoolyard game, Ramos.' I can hear him now."

"Let's worry about Reynolds later." Amy closed the door and propped the chair in front of it. "I believe I was in the middle of something important. Now, where was I?"

"Thighs. I distinctly remember you leaving just as you kissed my knees," Lucia said hopefully.

"Perhaps you're delirious with pain. But knees seem a perfectly good place to resume." Amy carefully pulled down the bedclothes and began to kiss Lucia's dark brown knees. "He could have killed you, my love."

"Higher."

"I don't know what I would do if I lost you."

"Less talk. More kissing, please."

Amy complied.

Photo by Tee Corinne

After a couple of grim decades in Texas, Mary Morell settled permanently in New Mexico. She and Anne Grey Frost, her partner in both business and pleasure, are enmeshed in their feminist bookstore, Full Circle Books. The store uses all the skills Mary learned as an English teacher, a counselor and a manager of travel agencies. For relaxation she picks up pretty rocks which she has agreed not to bring in the house. She also writes novels, poems, plays, political diatribes and occasional recipes. Her partner helps in the writing, but their two dogs, three cats and two horses do not.